WIDGMUS WORLD

WIDGMUS WORLD

A Sequel to *Gabriel's Magic Ornament*

Randall Bush

D.Phil., University of Oxford

BORDERSTONE PRESS, LLC

2011

First Edition

Widgmus World

Author: Randall Bush

Cover Art: D. Ellen Kay

Published by BorderStone Press, LLC,
PO Box 1383, Mountain Home, AR 72654
Dallas, TX - Memphis, TN

www.borderstonepress.com

© 2011 by Randall Bush

Supervising editor: Brian Mooney

ISBN: 978-1-936670-22-2

Library of Congress Control Number: 2011942705

Interior is acid free and lignin free.
It meets all ANSI standards for archival quality paper.

For my sisters, Susan and Donna

Table of Contents

—Chapter One—

BANG IN THE NIGHT

KIM RUSHED THROUGH the back door. "Mom, I'm home!" She slammed it shut, tossed her cap and muffler on the kitchen table, and flung her coat across a chair back. "Mom!" she called again.

Her younger brother Jason dawdled into the kitchen from the great room. "Too late. She's already done it."

"What?" Kim cried. She hurried from the kitchen into the great room with Jason trailing her.

Kim locked her eyes on the newly decorated Christmas tree. "Why couldn't you wait for us?"

Her mother turned, raised an eyebrow, and uttered calmly. "You and Jason weren't too interested in helping me yesterday, remember? The video games seemed more important, so I just assumed you were not interested."

"Look at the ornaments Mom used to decorate with," Jason grumbled. "They must have come from a garbage—ahem—*garage* sale."

Mom hurled a look of disapproval.

Kim sniggered. "What are they?"

"WidgWare," Mom uttered in a matter-of-a-fact tone. "They are the latest in holiday décor, and I think they're as cute as can be."

Kim walked over to the tree, removed one of the ornaments from a branch, and examined it as Jason stood by watching. "They look like globs of dried up play dough," he said under his breath.

Kim giggled, but Mom was not amused. "Really, Mom, they're hardly the right color for Christmas, are they? Halloween maybe. . ."

"Well, dried blood is red, and red is a Christmas color," Jason chimed in. He put his hands around his neck and acted out a death scene.

Mom shot him the evil eye. "Enough already!"

Meanwhile, Kim was checking out another ornament with her nose. "Mom," she said, "This stinks!" Her mother grabbed it and took a whiff.

"It's just your imagination!" she said. The expression on her face was clueless.

Jason, who had begun his own investigation, made a coughing, gagging noise. "Peeuwee!" He held it by the string like a dead mouse by its tail and handed it to Kim for her verdict.

Kim drew it cautiously to her nose, and then immediately jerked it away. "Bologna sandwich?"

"Sure smells like one to me," Jason chirped.

"You've got to be kidding," said Mom, wrenching it out of his hands and sniffing it.

Meanwhile, Kim smelled another. "Vinegar and coffee?" she said handing it to Jason, who took a whiff and nodded his agreement.

"Give me that!" Mom demanded, grabbing it from Jason and holding it up to her nose. "I don't smell a thing. Really, you children's imaginations are just overactive."

"Maybe your smeller's underactive," Jason suggested.

"Oh, quit exaggerating, will you?" Mother countered. "I want no more talk about these ornaments. Whether you like them or not, they're on the tree and on the tree they will stay."

Kim and Jason hung their heads, sauntered over to the sofa, plopped down, and sank into the cushions with their arms folded.

After she endured few moments of their silent sulking, Mom finally said, "Oh, fiddle. You kids needn't act that way. Let's try to make the best of the situation. The tree can stand a few more decorations, and if you will stop being such bad sports, I'll let you help." She went to the dining table to fetch some plastic shopping bags of different sizes. From one she removed a carton filled with balloons and little cardboard bodies. "I didn't plan on putting these on the tree, but I don't see that they will clash too terribly with the décor." After blowing up one of the balloons, she tied its end and pulled it through a slot where the little body's neck was located. "See how easy this is? Inflatable Christmas ornaments! Who'd have ever thunk it?" Next, from a larger shopping bag she unloaded little green Styrofoam cones and boxes of green toothpicks. "And I think we can make little Christmas trees from these, too," she said.

Kim and Jason gave each other a puzzled look. Obviously Mom had not thought out what could happen if the balloons got too close to the toothpicks. Despite their worst fears, however, the children decided to humor her for the time being.

"Here," said Mom handing balloons to the children. "Blow these up while I show you how to make little miniature Christmas trees from the Styrofoam cones and toothpicks."

Kim and Jason started inflating the balloons and quickly got the hang of attaching them to the tiny cardboard pieces. They watched as their mother stuck the green toothpicks at a downward angle into the green Styrofoam cones. As she was trying to stick a toothpick in an upright position into the very top of the cone, however, she pricked her index finger. "Ouch," she cried, and sucked on her finger. "Hmmm, this may not have been such a good idea after all. I'll go to the garage and look for some gloves and needle-nose pliers."

When Mom was out of earshot, Jason said to Kim. "What is she thinking? They look more like porcupines than Christmas trees."

"Beats me," Kim replied, giggling. "But I think we'd better go along with her for now. I just wish Dad were here. I know he wouldn't like what she's done to the Christmas tree."

Mom popped back into the room. "Lucky me!" she exclaimed cheerfully. "Two pairs of garden gloves and two pairs of pliers!" She distributed them to the children.

Kim, Jason, and their mother worked on assembling the balloon ornaments and toothpick Christmas trees all afternoon. Near dinner time, Mom took a break to go get burgers and fries. When she returned, they quickly emptied the sacks and ate at the coffee table. When they had finished, they continued their projects. Making the toothpick trees proved to be more time consuming than assembling the balloon ornaments, but at about 8:00 in the evening they were finished and were ready to start hanging their homemade ornaments on the tree.

"We've got to keep the toothpick trees separate from the little balloon people," said Mom. "We don't want their big old heads to pop." The children rolled their eyes at one another when she wasn't looking. "Hindsight is always better than foresight, I suppose," she continued. "We'll just have to be careful and space them so that the balloons are safe."

The children hung their homemade ornaments on the tree, and Mom supervised. By about 9:00 they had finished. Fortunately, they had not yet had a single balloon mishap.

"That should do it," said Mom, placing the last balloon ornament on the tree. "And the tree doesn't look too bad either, does it?"

The children felt no need to answer her. They were still not terribly thrilled about the strange ornaments their mother had picked out for their tree.

"My, it's getting late," Mom said looking at her watch. "Help me clean this mess up before bed."

"Oh, Mom," said Kim, "Can't we do it tomorrow? I'm tired."

"Too tired to play video games?" said Mom.

"Oh, okay," Kim relented.

The children quickly cleaned up so that they could play their video games. By 10:00 they had taken their baths and were in their pajamas. Mom exchanged "good nights" with them, and soon they were asleep.

* * *

Sometime during the wee hours of the morning, Mom and the children were awaked by a loud bang. "Kids! Are you okay?" Mom shouted from her bedroom.

Kim and Jason stumbled into the hallway, squinting and rubbing their eyes.

"What was that?" asked Jason.

"It sounded like a gunshot," said Kim.

"Stay close," said Mom, putting her arms around their shoulders. They proceeded fearfully and cautiously down the hallway. Suddenly the phone rang causing them to jump and let out a scream.

"Oh, gosh," said Mom patting her heart. "That's probably one of the neighbors calling." She hurried to the phone. The frightened children were clutching her robe.

As Mom picked up the receiver, her hands were shaking. "Hello?" There was a pause. "Yes, this is Janet Jeffery...Who? Yes. . .yes. . .yes," she nervously repeated as she held her right hand on her heart. Then there was a frightened, "What?"

From the look in Mom's eyes, the children knew something was wrong. "Who is it?" and "What's the matter?" kept coming like rapid fire from their mouths.

Mom covered the mouthpiece of the receiver long enough to quiet them, and then went back to listening intently. "Oh, no!" she whispered, covering her mouth. Her eyes filled with tears. "Are you sure?"

The children were now yanking on her nightgown, miming, and mouthing words without speaking. "One minute, please," she said to the person on the line and then looked squarely into the children's faces.

"Dad's been shot, but he's okay," she told them. "It was a flesh wound in his shoulder. They've already done surgery on him, and he's going to be fine." She went back to her phone conversation. "When will I be able to talk to him?" There was a long pause punctuated by an occasional "yes."

Then Mom said, "I can hardly believe it! That is wonderful news!"

"What? What?" the antsy children kept whispering as they tugged at her robe.

Mom covered the receiver again. "Dad's coming home for Christmas!"

The children started jumping up and down and broke into shouts of "yeah! yeah!" as they did.

"Quiet, children," said Mom. They continued to jump up and down but now merely whispered "yeah! yeah!"

"Yes," Mom continued on the phone. "Yes, we'll be here to receive his call. Thank you very much," and she hung up.

"Now," said Mom, smiling at the children. She crouched, leapt up with a loud "yeah!" and started jumping up and down like a cheerleader. She grabbed the children's hands, and they did a little celebration jig to the chant "Daddy's coming home for Christmas! Daddy's coming home for Christmas!"

"Okay, children," she finally said breathlessly. "Daddy will be calling tomorrow morning. I know with all this excitement, it will be hard to go back to sleep, but we've got to try. We've got quadrillions to do before he gets here."

Jason's face turned serious. "Mom, could the sound that woke us up be the gunshot that hit Dad?"

"The gunshot!" Mom exclaimed. "I almost forgot. There's no way we could have heard that, Jason."

"But we could have dreamed it," said Kim. "Doesn't that happen sometimes when people you love are in danger?"

Mom did not seem to hear Kim. She was staring at the wall. Her eyes widened, and she said, "Good heavens!"

"What?" Kim asked. Mom pointed at the wall.

The three of them walked over to it and stared at it silently. Jason reached up and pulled out a green toothpick.

"One of the balloon people must have popped," Kim guessed.

"I think you're right, Kim," said Mom.

"Wow. The wall looks like it got attacked by a crazy porcupine," Jason remarked.

"I can't believe one little balloon is responsible for ruining my pretty wall," said Mom. "It's a good thing we weren't in the room when it happened. Maybe we should take down the balloon and toothpick ornaments."

"No," said Jason. "We worked too hard to make them."

"Maybe it's just a freak accident," said Mom. "Anyway, we don't need to worry about it at 2:30 in the morning. Tomorrow will be a busy day, so we've got to get some sleep. Maybe tomorrow we will have time to make some alterations with the ornaments. We could always snip off the ends of the toothpicks so they won't be so sharp."

Mom and the children returned to bed and once again exchanged their "good nights." Despite all the excitement they had been through, they eventually drifted back to sleep.

* * *

The next morning, Janet sat at the kitchen table eating breakfast and thumbing through a recipe book. Though she tried to occupy her mind with finding recipes for Daryl's homecoming, she was on pins and needles as she awaited his phone call. The children were still asleep, for Janet had decided not to wake them due to the events of the night before.

At about 8:00 a.m. the phone finally rang, and Janet sprang up and answered it. "Hello."

"Janet, it's Daryl. How are you, sweetheart?"

The children, who were awakened by the phone, came running into the kitchen, so Janet put the phone on speaker.

"Daryl! We've been worried to death. Are you all right?"

"I'm fine. The wound was not life-threatening. I only had to have local anesthetic to remove the bullet. How are the kids?"

"They're right here," said Janet.

"Hi, Daddy," said Kim, "are you okay? We were worried."

"Yes, sweetheart, I'm fine."

"Hi, Dad," said Jason. "Dad, we heard the shot when you got hit! It woke us up."

"Jason," Mom said. "A balloon popped, remember?"

"What's that?" asked Daryl.

"Oh, honey, it's too long a story to go into now," said Janet. "Kids, let me talk to Dad a few minutes. You can listen in." Janet sat down in the chair by the phone.

"Janet, do my mom and dad know what happened?"

CHAPTER ONE

"I was waiting until you called me so I would know for sure you are all right."

"Good," said Daryl. "There was no use waking them up in the middle of the night. Call and tell them I'm okay, and tell them I'll be calling them soon."

"I'll call them as soon as I get off the phone with you," said Janet. "Now, tell us what happened."

"It's the strangest thing, Janet," Daryl began. "We had a very tense standoff yesterday here in Bethlehem. Kidnappers were holding an old Palestinian woman hostage inside the Church of the Nativity. We had been stationed outside the church all night. Everything seemed pretty quiet. Then, about three in the morning, I saw something gold glittering in a pile of burning rubbish. I didn't think there would be any harm in retrieving it from the fire, so I crawled over to the fire, wrapped my bandana around my hand, grabbed the object, and stuffed it into my knapsack. I had barely done this when gunfire erupted. When I saw a trail of dust raised by one of their bullets, I realized they were firing at me. Before I could get out of range, I felt warm liquid oozing down my right arm. Then I realized I'd been hit in the shoulder and was bleeding. Anyway, I passed out. Later, when I came to, I was being rushed by medics to the hospital. By then, the shoulder was really hurting, so they gave me something for the pain. I've been out most of the day."

"Daryl, why didn't you leave whatever thing that was in the fire?"

"I'm glad I didn't," said Daryl. "The object was a golden angel. When I removed it from my knapsack, I discovered its wing had been severed, and I knew why. The angel lost its wing because the bullet that hit me hit it first. The angel deflected the bullet away from my heart and into my shoulder. If it hadn't been for that angel, I would be dead."

"But if you hadn't tried to remove it from the fire, maybe you wouldn't have gotten shot at in the first place," said Janet. "Wait a minute, Daryl. The kids want to talk to you again."

"Hey, Dad."

"Hey, Jason."

"Dad, are you going to bring the golden angel home when you come?"

"I surely will, Jason," he said. "It is, after all, my lucky guardian angel. Its wing is being repaired right now."

"Dad?"

"Yes, Kim."

"Maybe we can use your lucky angel as a Christmas ornament when you come."

"Yeah, Dad," Jason piped in. "The Christmas tree really needs it. Mother has decorated it with ugly ornaments. Some of the ornaments are dangerous, too."

"Janet, what on earth is he talking about?"

"Daryl, you don't need to worry about that now. I'll explain later."

"Oh, darling," said Daryl. "The nurse has just walked in so I need to go for now. I don't have access to a computer here, but I'll email the flight information as soon as I can."

"Wonderful, honey," said Janet. "I love you."

"Love you, too, sweetheart."

"Bye, Dad," Kim and Jason said.

"Bye, kids," Dad said. "I love you and will be seeing you soon."

—Chapter Two—

HOME FOR CHRISTMAS

GRANDPA DROVE THE FAMILY to the airport in the minivan on Thursday afternoon to pick up Daryl. Jason sat up front with Grandpa so that Grandma, Mom, and Kim could sit in the backseat and chat. When they arrived at the airport, Grandma decided to circle the airport in the minivan while the kids, Grandpa, and Janet went inside to meet Daryl and help him with his luggage. They all waited anxiously at the exit from customs. When Kim and Jason caught sight of their dad coming through the exit, they started jumping up and down. Janet and Grandpa waved vigorously. When Dad pushed through the glass doors, the children ran, leapt up, hugged, and kissed him.

"Ouch! Careful, Jason," Dad said, protecting his hurt shoulder.

"Jason!" Mom scolded.

"It's okay," Daryl said, kneeling down and hugging Jason and Kim with his good arm and giving them each a kiss. "Good to see you, kiddos." He stood up and hugged Janet. "I'm so glad to see you, darling."

"We're so glad you're home," said Janet.

Then Daryl hugged Grandpa.

"Hello, Son," Grandpa greeted him.

"It's good to see you, Dad. Where's Mom?"

"She's circling the airport in the car. We thought it would be easier than having to park and take your luggage all that way."

Janet hugged Daryl again. "I can't tell you how good it is to hold you at last," she whispered. "You have no idea how worried we all were."

"We can put that nightmare behind us now," said Daryl. "All that matters now is that I'm here, and I'm feeling great. I just want to get home and enjoy being with my family."

"Son, let me help you with your bags," said Grandpa, hoisting Daryl's backpack over his shoulder.

"Thanks, Dad," Daryl said.

"We'd better not keep your mother waiting," said Grandpa.

They squeezed their way through the bustling airport to passenger pickup.

"There's the minivan," said Grandpa. "I'll load the luggage. Jason and Kim, you can help me if you want."

When Grandma caught sight of Daryl, she sprang out of the front seat, rushed over, hugged him, and planted a sloppy wet kiss on his cheek. "My sweet boy," she said, clutching him. Then she started crying.

"That's okay, Mom," he said, hugging her. "I'm safe now. And I'm home."

She removed a tissue from her purse and dabbed the tears from her eyes. "We are so proud of you, Daryl. We were worried sick, of course, especially after we heard you had been wounded. But we are so very proud of you. I hope you never have to face danger like that again. I can't stand even to think about it. I love you, Son." She gave him another big hug.

"Same here, Mom. I'm so glad to be home."

"I'll tell you one thing," Daryl's mother said. "We are going to celebrate the heck out of Christmas this year. I've been cooking up a storm. My kitchen looks like a hurricane hit it."

"Did you make any of your famous chocolate pies?" asked Daryl.

"Are you kidding? What kind of mother do you think I am?"

Just then Jason came running up. "Dad, Grandpa has your bags loaded. He says we'd better leave the parking area before the airport police get on to us."

They walked over to the minivan, and Grandma opened the back door. "Daryl, you go ahead and sit in the back with Janet and the kids, and I'll ride up front with your father."

They meandered their way out of the airport and soon were headed home. Grandpa drove, and Daryl told the family what had happened on the night he had taken the bullet in his shoulder. In time, he drifted to the story of the golden angel he had found glittering in the fire.

"I call it 'my lucky angel,'" he said. "When I saw it sparkling in that fire, I couldn't resist finding out what it was, so I wrapped my bandana around my hand, reached in to the fire, and pulled it out. Now I'm not sure whether I rescued it or it rescued me. It's a miracle that the bullet ricocheted off the angel's wing and missed my heart."

"Where is the angel? Can we see it?" asked Kim.

"It's with my things. I'll show it to you when we get home," he replied. "Anyway, what I didn't know at the time was the great value of what I'd found. When I finally did remove it from my pack and saw that its wing was bent, I tried to straighten it, but the wing broke off. The bullet had already pretty much severed the wing. So I asked one of my men to take it in to repair it. He took it to a tinker in the Old City. For many years, the tinker had made golden angels very much like the one I'd found. Now this is where the story gets really interesting. The next day, the tinker paid me a special visit in the hospital. With him was a man who introduced himself as the Patriarch of Jerusalem. As the tinker talked to me, he was greatly excited."

As Dad told the children the story, he tried to mimic the tinker's speech. "'This is the angel of miracles! When he have his wing put back, I know he be special. When I repair him, his wings, they flap! The angel—he turn white! He shine like Star of Bethlehem! And he do so quick! Flash! When I repair wing, a miracle happen! Then I look. I no see place where I repair it! It have no seam—'tis perfect—like the day it was made. Is a miracle, I say! A miracle!"

"Then the Patriarch of Jerusalem chimed in," Dad continued. As he did, he tried to speak in a foreign accent. "'The tinker, he makes many golden angels like this one, but this—this is the first—the real—the true angel the Bishop of Myra made long, long ago. He made it from gold the Wise Man Balthasar bring to the Holy Christ Child. We are sure now this is the angel of miracles. He goes into the world time and again only to fly back to the Holy Church of the Nativity once his task is done. He is the angel of enchanted Christmas dreams—the one they call Gabriel. He is placed under your care for a time! But only a time, for he is free. Free as the wind. It is true. He gives the gift he chooses to give, and what gift is that? No one can tell. Treat this angel with much care, for you did not choose to find it. He chose to find you!"

"Wow, that's so cool!" Jason exclaimed, interrupting Dad's story. "May we hang it on the Christmas tree when we get home? Please?"

"That's exactly what I had in mind," said Dad. "You and Kim can do it together if you want. But don't be too disappointed if nothing happens. The Patriarch and the tinker might just have been telling one of those old Middle-Eastern legends. I don't doubt they believed what they told me was true. Still, it is fun to make believe, right?"

"I'm not sure anyone can make believe after what Mom has done to the Christmas tree," said Kim.

"Kim, do we have to go there?" Mom interrupted. "The ornaments are just fine!"

Daryl looked at Janet.

"Nuh-uh," Kim and Jason uttered.

"Stop it this very minute, children. You two have made such a big deal about the way I've decorated the tree this year." She spoke to Daryl. "I've decorated the tree in a new line of ornaments known as WidgWare, and the children can't stop telling me how much they hate them. But WidgWare is the latest style, and everyone is using them because they are inexpensive and cute."

"Cute," said Jason. "They look like vomit and dried up blood!"

"Jason! Mind your tongue!" Mom scolded.

"Well, they do. And there are exploding ornaments on the tree, too," he added.

"Oh, for heaven's sake," said Mom. "We made little balloon people and toothpick trees," she explained to Daryl, "and they got a little too close. I'm sure we'll be able to fix the problem without too much difficulty."

"I'm sure Mom's decorating taste isn't as bad as you kids are making out," said Dad.

"Oh, the WidgWare *is* so cute, you'll see," said Mom. "I'm sure you will agree when you see it." Then Mom looked at the children. "And I'm sure you two will learn to love it, too, right?"

The kids just hung their heads.

"Home again, home again, jiggety-jig" said Grandpa, rolling into the driveway and coming to a halt.

The children jumped out of the car's back seat and hurried to its trunk. When Grandpa opened it using the automatic latch next to his seat, the kids fought to get to Dad's knapsack.

"What's the matter with you children?" said Grandma, coming around to the trunk. "Your Dad has barely gotten home, and you're already quarrelling."

"Which bag has the angel?" Kim asked eagerly.

"Oh, that's it," said Dad with a smile. "Okay, everybody help me get these bags into the house. I promise we'll locate the angel first thing."

The kids and Grandpa each grabbed a piece of luggage and carried them into the house. Dad, Mom, and Grandma followed. When Dad entered the house, the kids were jumping up and down. "Where is it? Where is it?"

Dad rummaged through the knapsack, removed the ornament, and held it up. The kids' eyes glowed with excitement. Then they started jumping up to try to get the ornament out of Dad's hand.

"Hold your horses!" said Dad, keeping it out of their reach. "I've got to take a look at this Christmas tree to see if it looks as ugly as you say. I don't know if we will want to put such a beautiful ornament on a tree that looks too ugly."

Dad walked over the tree to investigate the WidgWare decorations. "Hmmm. Interesting."

"You see?" said Jason. "They *are* ugly."

Daryl looked at the tree for a while, and then said, "Well, they are...*different*."

"You don't like them either?" Janet asked disappointedly.

"I like them if you do, dear," he said, kissing her. "All right, kids, you can go ahead and put the angel on the tree."

"Yippee!" they shouted, as he handed it to them.

* * *

Kim and Jason hung the ornament on the tree next to a garland of tinsel. The minute it touched, a very odd thing happened. A swirl of golden sparkles suddenly surrounded the children. Each sparkle gradually lengthened and grew larger as Kim's and Jason's bodies began to shrink.

"Kim? Mom? Dad? Where are you?" shouted Jason.

"Here I am!" Kim exclaimed.

"I can hear you," said Jason, "but I can't see you."

"Same here," Kim said.

The children kept calling for their mother and father, but their parents did not answer.

"I don't hear them," said Jason. "Oh no, now I'm having trouble breathing."

"Me, too," said Kim, gasping. "Grandpa! Grandma! Mom! Dad! Please help us!" The kids shouted as loud as they could, but their parents and grandparents were silent. The golden sparkles kept getting thicker.

"What is this stuff?" Jason said, gagging. "It's harder and harder to breathe."

"The sparkles are turning into some kind of fizzy water," Kim shouted. "We've got to hold our breath—Jason!"

They thrashed madly through the fizzy water, desperate to find a way out. When their heads finally surfaced, they were coughing.

"My eyes really burn," cried Jason, trying to open them.

"Mine, too," shouted Kim, squinting. "What was that stuff we went through? Where are we?"

They rubbed their eyes and finally were able to see that they were caught in the current of an eerie looking canal. Its water was dark, though its surface glimmered with gold-colored streaks.

"Are you okay, Jason?" Kim shouted, panting and treading water.

"Yeah, I think so," he said, still coughing and trying to catch his breath. He struggled to stay afloat.

"Look!" she said signaling. "The shore's over there. Let's swim for it."

Dogpaddling toward the river bank, they soon managed to free themselves from the current and were able to grip the slimy river bottom with their toes, making it possible to wade ashore.

"This goo is disgusting," said Kim, wading through it. "It's in my shoes and between my toes."

"This whole place really stinks," said Jason, wheezing. "Just like some of those ornaments we smelled."

"The odor must be coming from those fizzy bubbles," replied Kim. "It smells like rotten eggs."

"Look at them when they pop," said Jason. "The awful yellow fog is coming from inside them. Where are the bubbles coming from?"

"It beats me," replied Kim, "and I don't think it would be smart to stay around and find out."

Kim and Jason finally managed to climb onto the bank of the canal.

"Well, I think Dad's ornament worked," supposed Kim. "Dad was wrong about it being only a legend. But why would it bring us to such a horrible and disgusting place."

"It stinks so bad," said Jason, "and in more ways than one."

"Right," Kim agreed. "This is all very, very strange if you ask me. You know, when you look at those bubbles from the shore, they aren't as yellow looking. They look a bit gray-green, don't you think?"

"I'd hate to think what Mom would say if she knew we were swimming in that goop. I'll bet it's full of pollution. I hope our skin doesn't rot off."

"How disgusting," Kim commented. "Gosh, I'd love a bath about now."

"I would, too," said Jason. "That slimy mud from the river bottom feels like worms squiggling between my toes."

Kim looked around her. "This place gives me the creeps. I hope we can find our way back home and quick."

"Look at that," said Jason, pointing to an object, "what could it be?" They walked over to it.

"A sign of some sort, I think," replied Kim. "It says a quarter of a mile, but to what? All I can see is a squiggly line."

"What do you think it means?" asked Jason.

"A snake? A streak of lightning, perhaps?" Kim ventured to guess.

"Maybe there's some kind of electrical danger ahead," said Jason.

"At this point that actually would come as no surprise," Kim remarked. "But at least this does look like some kind of a road. I suppose we should follow it and see where it leads."

They followed the road, but soon found that it led into a dead forest. The trees had branches like broom straw. All the leaves had fallen off, and the broom straw was covered with mold, mildew, and glistening spider webs.

"What happened here, I wonder?" Kim asked.

"A nuclear leak, probably," said Jason.

"I bet this forest is haunted," said Kim. "There could be dangerous ghosts lurking in those trees."

"If you're trying to scare me, Kim, it won't work!" Jason said.

Kim just then caught sight of a grayish-yellow object through the trees. "Oh? And what could that be?" she said, making her voice tremble. "Is that a ghost? Wooooo!"

"I'm not scared," said Jason, "so you can just stop wasting your breath."

Kim began walking toward the object with Jason trailing. "Are you thinking what I'm thinking?" asked Kim.

"I would recognize it anywhere," said Jason. "That looks just like Mom's WidgWare."

"Exactly!" said Kim. "Except it's a gigantic version. I can even smell the vinegar and strong coffee from here. Jason, do you know where we are? We are inside our Christmas tree!"

"Oh, great," said Jason. "Now we have to deal with WidgWare in a whole new way!"

"Dad's lucky guardian angel must have brought us here," said Kim.

"Yeah," Jason said. "It sure would have been nice to redecorate the tree first. Now we're stuck with Mom's wonderful world of WidgWare!"

"Some *lucky angel*," Kim stated sarcastically. "Look. There's another of those strange lightning marks. What could they mean?"

"They look sort of scary, if you ask me," Jason replied. "Maybe we should get out of these woods. I'm starting to get a bad feeling about this place."

The children turned to head back toward the river, but were startled and frightened when a voice behind them screeched, "Very Widgmus!"

Panic flashed out of Jason's eyes. "What's that?"

"I think it came from the WidgWare," Kim answered.

"This place gives me the creeps. Let's leave *now*," Jason whispered.

They started running down the road. Through the trees, they could see more of the WidgWare objects. Some were colored burnt orange. Others were mud-red and brownish-green. They could smell bologna sandwiches and other nauseating odors. The WidgWare seemed to be frosted not with snow but with some kind of mold or mildew. They all had lightning marks inscribed on them like the ones they'd seen earlier.

Eventually, as Kim and Jason approached a clearing, they heard whirring motors and loud stamping. Stamp! Whir! Stamp! Whir! Louder and louder it got. Not far ahead they caught sight of a ramshackle factory. Brown smoke, which smelled like sulfur, billowed and puffed from its smokestacks—about six in all. The siding and roof of the building were made of rusted, corrugated tin. Streaming in and out of it were odd elf-like creatures dressed in what appeared at first to be Santa suits. A closer look, however, revealed that the suits were the color of dried blood with trim that could have easily passed for rat fur. Kim and Jason drew closer, and kept out of the creatures' line of sight.

Their misshapen faces, the color of mud, were missing different features. Either they had too many noses, eyes, mouths, and ears, or not enough. If this were not bad enough, their features were not in their normal places either. One had arms that branched out like tree limbs, and his hands had what looked like worms instead of fingers. Though the hands belonged to the same creature, the hands were fighting one another. As one hand would launch an attack, the offended hand would retaliate. The creature itself, however, observed his own hands fighting like a spectator would at an arm-wrestling match. He would cheer on one hand and boo the other as though one of the hands really did not belong to him at all.

"*What* is *that*?" asked Jason.

Kim was speechless.

Another creature had spindly legs, but the feet these legs were attached to were frogs which each had four separate legs as well. To get around, the creature would shout "hop!" at one of its frog feet. When both feet would start hopping, the creature would shout at the other foot, "not *you, you!*" Unfortunately the feet would seem to get more and more confused with every command. Meanwhile, the creature would try to keep his balance like a rider on a mad bronco bull. Sometimes, the feet would hop without warning, taking the creature by surprise, hopping out from under it and causing it to fall flat on its face or on its back.

Kim and Jason hid in bushes and watched this extremely odd spectacle. Then a voice from behind frightened them.

"Who *you*?" The voice sounded like fingernails scratching a chalkboard. They turned and feasted their eyes on a creature with a face that looked very much like a mole's. But its mouth had long, sharp, and uneven fangs. Instead of fingers, it had webbed claws, and its scaly feet had large, swollen toes. "You be in the forbidden forest!" it slobbered. "What business have you here? You wish to buy R.A.A.P.?"

When the creature said 'R. A. A. P.' he pronounced it 'rap'.

"Yes, I guess that's what we're here for," said Kim, thinking quickly on her feet. "Rap."

"You *guess*?" the creature interrogated. "Either you here for R.A.A.P. or you not. And if you not, then *why* you here at all."

"What is *rap*?" asked Jason. Kim poked him in the ribs with her elbow to shut him up.

The creature let out a screech when Jason asked him the question, and the other creatures came running, hobbling, and hopping toward them. Kim and Jason turned tail and ran, but the creature with the frog legs managed to get his feet to cooperate long enough to propel his body over their heads so that he landed directly in front of them and uttered the word, "Checkmate!"

When the other creatures had them surrounded, the creature with the mole face marched up to them and stuck its nose in their faces. "You shall be escorted to Queen Lady, you will," he said. "She will punish you for trespassing in her royal forest."

"Queen Lady, who?" asked Jason. Kim rolled her eyes. She couldn't believe Jason had introduced a "lady, who?" joke at a time like this. She stepped on his toes to shut him up. "Owww!" he cried, but Kim just glared at him.

"Fine," said Kim. "Take us to Queen Lady, whoever she is. You don't have to threaten us, you know, and you don't have to be rude."

"Threaten us? Be rude?" screamed the mole-faced creature. "You are not us! Do you hear? Widgmudgeons only threaten enemies of Queen Lady! You must be her enemy, or we would not threaten you!" The children could only guess what the Mole-Faced One meant by this peculiar logic.

"We don't know who Queen Lady is," said Kim. "How can we be her enemy?"

"Horror!" screeched the Mole-Faced One. "They know not our Queen Lady!" The other creatures were thrown into a panic and kept saying, "They know her not! They know her not!"

The Mole-Faced One shushed them. "How can such a thing be?" he said.

"You are not very nice elves," Kim said. These words sent them into even greater frenzy. "Elves!" cried the Mole-Faced One, cringing. "They speak of elves!" The other creatures carried on something fierce. The Mole-Faced One pointed at Kim and Jason and screamed, "Enemy! Enemy!"

"I'm sorry," Kim apologized. "If you aren't elves, then what are you?"

"Royal Widgmudgeons of the Order of Homunculi," he yelled back. "You know nothing at all, strange beings!"

"Oh, yes, I should have known you were Royal Mishmashes of the Order of Uncle Homer. . .," said Kim, trying to calm him. "Anyone with half a brain would know that."

"You know nothing of Widgmudgeons or Homunculi, I presume?" the Widgmudgeon stated. "You are not a creator, then!"

"What do you mean?" Kim asked.

"You know not?" it screamed back. "The strange creature knows not! Take her to Queen Lady! Now!"

"How forgetful of me," Kim announced. "I *am* a creator, of course, just as you say." The truth was that she couldn't understand these creatures. They scared her, so she thought it best to try to humor them for the time being.

"Creators don't forget such things!" the Mole-Faced One shouted with a cold stare. "You lie."

"What is your name?" asked Jason.

"The other strange being speaks!" said the Mole-Faced One, glaring at him. "You are a trickster? You desire my name? Indeed, you shall have it not! If you are a creator, you would know my name, but you are one who knows it not and never shall!" Then the Mole-Faced One said to the many-handed Widgmudgeon. "Tie them up, Strike!"

"Aha!" said Kim. "Now we know your friend's name is Strike!"

"You are one who knows not!" shouted the Mole-Faced One. "We call him Strike to fool the enemy. You of little knowledge will be scared when you get where you're going!" Then he shouted at Strike, "Put restrainers on the strange beings!" and with that, Strike's fingers reeled out from his many hands and tied themselves in knots around Kim and Jason's bodies.

"Let me go!" shouted Jason, struggling to break free.

"Be still! Shut thy trap!" warned Strike with an evil gleam in his eye, "or wormy fingers will grow tight and squeeze you to death."

"To Queen Lady with these!" exclaimed the Mole-Faced One. "These will pay for messing with R.A.A.P. production!"

With that command, the throng of Widgmudgeons began marching down the road with their prisoners.

—Chapter Three—

THE *BABY LONNIE*

KIM AND JASON MARCHED down the path, and Strike's fingers held them tight, guiding them in the direction he chose. They could hardly believe such a small creature possessed such enormous strength. In time they arrived at the banks of the river they had escaped from earlier.

"Into the boat with them," said the Mole-Faced One. The Widgmudgeon throng obeyed. Soon they were pushing away from shore. In time, Kim and Jason caught sight of a large river boat anchored in the middle of the river.

"What is that?" asked Jason.

"The *Baby Lonnie*," said the Mole-Faced One with a look of delight. "Queen Lady ever glides in her river palace cruiser down her beauteous Tinsel canals." His expression underwent an abrupt change, and he looked temporarily angelic. "But for you it no palace, but a prison, will be!"

"Do you have to be so mean?" Kim asked. "Whatever did we do to upset you?"

"Queen Lady will cause you to know in good time," replied the Mole-Faced One. "She knows all! She likes not her Widgmudgeons to be upset. She will scold you strange creatures and give you a bad punishment."

Kim and Jason became more and more nervous as they neared the palace cruiser. When they approached the port side of the riverboat, the Mole-Faced One screeched, "Widgmudgeons, ahoy!"

A harsh voice shot back from the deck, "You had better have a good reason for coming here!"

"We got prisoners for Queen Lady," the Mole-Faced One uttered. "Milady will be greatly pleased and so greatly happy."

"We'll see about that," the voice returned. "You have permission to board, but be sure to wipe your feet. Queen Lady cannot stand Widgmudgeon slime on her decks."

They hoisted Strike, the Mole-Faced One, and the children up with ropes on pulleys while the other Widgmudgeons climbed up a rope ladder. When the children reached the ship's deck, a large, hunchbacked sailor squinted at them. His eyes were deep and dark, and he had black, bushy eyebrows. He wore a dirty orange and yellow striped suit and a drab, green cap. "Wait here," he ordered with a gruff voice. "Queen Lady will be told of your arrival." With those words, the sailor left them.

"You strange creatures in bad trouble," the Mole-Faced One gloated with an evil grin. "You will see soon how much trouble."

Several moments later, the sailor returned. "Queen Lady has agreed to receive you," he informed them. "Follow me."

After trudging down a long corridor, they entered a large, gaudily furnished room. A large woman was sitting on an immense, pink sofa. Her pink dress, which clung close to her pudgy body, was covered with orange sequins, and she wore a long cape covered with pink sequins that did not match well the color of her sofa.

"What are you Widgmudgeons doing here?" she interrogated. "You know you are forbidden to be seen on the *Baby Lonnie*!"

"But Queen Lady," said the Mole-Faced One. "We found spies. They are creatures not of our world! They are creatures who know not!"

"You will leave this ship at once!" she shouted. "Homunculus Wermivilangese," she said to Strike. A look of horror flew across his face because she had spoken his real name. "Take your slimy fingers off these precious children!" He obeyed and cowered in fear. Kim and Jason were relieved to be set free.

"Now get off this boat at once, you river scum, or I will teach you lessons you shall never forget!"

The Widgmudgeons scampered away, and Queen Lady walked over to comfort the children. "You poor, poor little things," she said. "You must excuse them. Had I known you had come to visit Widgmus World, or that Widgmudgeons had taken you captive, I would have taken measures sooner."

"Widgmus World? Is that where we are?" asked Kim.

"Indeed, my dear child," replied Queen Lady. "And I am its Chief Executive Officer. Believe me, if I had known Widgmudgeons were pestering you, I could have put on my cyberbonnet and scattered them like fluff."

"*Cyber-vomit?*" asked Jason.

"Cyber*bonnet*," she corrected him, chuckling. "It's a device I use to control them," replied Queen Lady. "They are nasty little creatures, true, but they are useful. Wait here and I'll show you how the cyberbonnet works." She left and soon returned with a helmet that started glittering with psychedelic colors when she placed it on her head.

"I am punishing them now for being rude to you," Queen Lady said. "I promise they shall not bother you again."

"How does it work?" Jason asked.

"It connects my thoughts to the wire ways of the Wonderful World of Widgmus. Indeed, I can control my whole empire from this very sofa. It's much easier than having to travel."

"Is that why they call you Queen Lady?" asked Kim.

"Oh, my dear," she said, batting her eyes. "Don't flatter me. I wouldn't exactly use *that* word for what I do. Really, I'm just an ordinary person who has taken upon herself responsibility for the Widgmus World beautification project. Maybe you children have seen some of my fabulous creations?"

"You mean the Widgmudeons?" asked Kim.

"Oh, no," she replied. "Well, true, I did create them, but they are only my support staff. Here, let me show you."

Queen Lady exited the room and in a few moments returned with a gray-green object that looked like a large glob of snot.

"That's WidgWare," Jason commented.

"Then you *have* seen my fine artwork?" said Queen Lady.

"Yes, our whole Christmas tree is decorated with it," said Jason without a hint of enthusiasm.

"Your mother must have extremely fine taste, then," she uttered with a glint of pride in her eyes.

"We've always thought so," said Kim. "But. . ."

"Then you must tell your mother that you met Verbada Widgmud. I am *the* Verbada Widgmud, of course—Senior Designer and Chief Executive Officer of WidgWare Incorporated."

"What exactly *is* WidgWare?" asked Jason.

"You really don't know, do you, you poor little thing," remarked Verbada. "That is really inexcusable. My publicists are falling down on the job again!" She made a quick phone call. "Give me Quirinius Grousenot! This minute!" She paused and winked at the children. "Grousenot?" she barked. "Is that you?" She paused as he spoke to her. "Yes, fine, thank you." She said to him. They could vaguely hear him chattering on the other side of the line. "Yes, Grousenot. Now listen carefully. I have two children from very deprived circumstances who know virtually nothing about

WidgWare." Again there was a pause. "Yes, exactly. I could hardly believe it either. These children need the tour as soon as possible." She paused again. "Yes, it's a must, and today, do you hear?" Again she paused. "Yes, that is a wonderful idea. A visit to the production studio would be perfect. Now, I want you to give the word to Captain Rushport to crank the *Baby Lonnie* into high gear." She paused, said "Thank you, Grousenot," and hung up the phone.

"You children are in for a real treat," Verbada informed them. Not many folks in Widgmus World are fortunate enough to be taken on a guided tour, much less a tour on the *Baby Lonnie* herself. You will soon see wonders beyond your wildest dreams. But enough talk for now about my magnificent corporation. The Widgmudgeons were right about one thing. You children are obviously among 'those who do not know'. All I can figure out is that you children must be new to Widgmus World."

"You are right," said Kim. "We placed our dad's lucky angel ornament on the Christmas tree. That's how we got here."

Shock flashed across Verbada's face. "I can't believe your mother would ruin a perfectly good Widgmus tree by letting you put a foreign object on it, even if it was lucky as your father claims."

"Well, Mom really wasn't responsible," said Kim. "It was Dad who gave us the idea."

"That figures," said Verbada. "Leave it to a man to ruin the effect of a perfectly decorated Widgmus tree. Wherever did he find that old thing, anyway? Have you any idea?"

"Outside of an old church in Bethlehem," Jason answered.

Verbada seemed horrified, and mumbled something. Then she asked the children. "What else do you children know of this ornament? Did your father tell you stories about it? Did he perchance tell you its name?"

"No," said Kim. "He only told us that it was his lucky guardian angel."

"I find that hard to believe," Verbada commented. "Your father seems very superstitious. He didn't by chance mention anyone by the name of *Lady*, did he?"

"No, but aren't you Queen Lady?" Jason asked.

"Well, yes, of course I am, my dear boy," Verbada reassured him. "Who else could I be after all?" Then she changed the subject. "You children must be hungry. Would you like to try some of my delicious apple sours?"

"Goody," said the children, and they each popped one in their mouth. But when they started sucking them, their faces puckered up as though they had bitten right into a bitter lemon.

"Oh," said Verbada, noticing their expressions. "You're just not used to them yet. But you must believe me—they get sweeter each time you eat one. In time, you will just *love* them." Then she changed the subject. "Would you children like for me to tell you a wonderful story?"

"Yes," they said, perking up with excitement.

"I call this one of my 'once upon a no time' stories, because the whole tale I'm going to tell you is about something that never really happened. Do you understand?"

"Not really," said Jason.

"Then I shall try to explain," said Verbada. "Just sit here beside me on the sofa and suck on your apple sours while I tell it. The more you suck on the apple sours, the better you will understand."

Jason and Kim sat beside her as she began her tale. "Once upon a no time, there was not a little boy named Chris or a little girl named Laura, because Chris and Laura were never born. They were not real people, you see. And their father, who also was never born, was not a real person either. So he couldn't very well have brought home a magic ornament called Gabriel's Magic Ornament, could he have? Even if the ornament had been real, which, of course, it was not, Chris and Laura's father could not have brought it home to them. Do you children understand why he could not?"

"Because their father was never born?" replied Kim.

"Oh! I get it!" exclaimed Jason. "Nothing in the story ever really happened!"

"How smart you both are!" exclaimed Verbada. "You children are exceptionally gifted."

Jason and Kim sucked on the apple sour, and seemed to understand more and more clearly what Verbada was telling them.

"When Chris and Laura were carried into a place called Arboria—or I should say *were not* carried to *no* place that was *not* named Arboria—they did *not* meet a person named Lady. Do you know why they did not meet her?" Verbada asked.

"Because Chris and Laura were never born and there was no such person as Lady?" Jason replied.

"Precisely," Verbada replied. "Your intelligence quotients are off the charts!"

"But you are Queen Lady," said Jason. "Does that mean you are only half real?"

Verbada chuckled. "No, no, no, dear boy. The Lady I'm referring to is not me but another Lady. Or I should say, *not* another Lady since she never existed. They do call me *Queen* Lady, of course. But please don't confuse me with the Lady in my 'once upon a no time' story who never existed, all right?"

Jason nodded.

"Anyway," Verbada continued, "since that Lady was not real, she could not have very well warned Chris and Laura about a monstrous creature called Lesnit who ate angel stars, because Chris and Laura were never born, and there was never a creature called Lesnit, and there were never such things as angel stars. Do you children understand what I'm trying to tell you?"

"I think so," Kim replied.

"Good," said Verbada, "Most importantly, the monstrous creature who never existed and who was not called Lesnit did not try to devour any Star at Tree Top where someone named Tree King supposedly lived, because there was no Lesnit, no Star at Tree Top, and no Tree King."

"I'm getting mixed up now," said Jason.

"You will be all right," Verbada reassured him. "Just keep sucking on your apple sour. In time, you'll see things much more clearly."

Verbada rattled on and on with her 'no time' story. By the time she had finished, Kim and Jason no longer knew what to believe.

Finally Jason said, "Now let me get this straight. There really is no such thing as the lucky angel ornament that brought us here?"

"Now you're seeing things my way," said Verbada. "It's best now that you forgot how you got here. Most people forget that someone else was responsible for bringing them into the world, so it's best that you forget, too. Would you children like some more apple sours?"

Jason and Kim popped the sours in their mouths and continued to listen to more of Verbada's 'once upon a no time' stories. As Verbada promised, the apple sours seemed to get sweeter the more they ate, and the children found that they just couldn't stop eating them. At length, Verbada said, "Now it's time for you children to try to tell your own 'once upon a no time' stories."

"Let me!" Jason volunteered. "Once upon a no time, there was no such thing as Verbada Widgmud. . ."

"Jason," said Verbada. "Look me in the face. Can you not see that I am real?"

"Oh, I get it," he said. "A 'once upon a no time story' has to be about some made-up person."

"That's right," said Verbada. "I may very well be the only real thing left in Widgmus World. Just remember that."

"Are you saying the Widgmudgeons and the river with golden streaks aren't real?" asked Kim.

"We refer to the waterways in Widgmus World as Tinsel Canal," Verbada clarified. "They and the Widgmudgeons are real enough. That's all you need to know for now. Just believe what I tell you and never doubt my word. Otherwise, you may get lost along the way, and that would be terrible. I am going to be your guide on the most marvelous and extraordinary Tinsel Canal cruise two children have ever taken through Widgmus World! And best of all, you will come to know the true meaning of Widgmus on the way!"

"What exactly is Widgmus?" asked Jason.

"Why, it is my name for the holiday that used to be called Christmas!" said Verbada. "Just wait. I'm sure you'll just grow to *love* Widgmus even more than Christmas! Now," she said, "it's time that we climbed on deck. If you children are good, I'll let you help me with my next project."

Excited about their journey, Kim and Jason ran up the stairs that led to the deck, and soon Queen Lady Verbada Widgmud had joined them.

—Chapter Four—

R.A.A.P.

ON THE DECK, SAILORS dressed like jailbirds frantically mopped up Widgmudgeon slime tracks. The sailors' faces oozed with disgust, and they grumbled as they swabbed the deck. Their anger at the Widgmudgeons' mess had sharpened the pupils of their eyes to points, and their eyebrows squirmed like black fuzzy caterpillars crawling across hot concrete.

The *Baby Lonnie* paddled down Tinsel Canal, and passed town after town. Verbada's ugly WidgWare ornaments could be seen everywhere—in trees; on rooftops; hanging from poles along the shore like deformed and lightless Japanese lanterns; standing in front yards like garden gnomes that had gotten too close to an explosion; hanging from windows like slabs of bologna and pigs feet; strung from light pole to light pole like sausage links. The smell of garlic traveled on breezes carried from the towns onto Tinsel Canal and mingled there with the canal's normal smell of rotten eggs. With signs of Christmas nowhere visible, the towns looked bleak and forlorn.

"Isn't that little shanty town cute?" Verbada would ask while they were passing what seemed were heaps of cardboard boxes, taped together but warped from rain.

She pointed. "There's another cute little village that has gone all out for WidgWare. How brilliant their Town Council must be to enact Widgmus legislation." Straggly-haired folks wearing rags gathered on the docks as the *Baby Lonnie* paddled past. While a few waved unenthusiastically as Verbada's river cruiser crept by, others simply stared in their direction from hollow eyes. "What good taste they have," Verbada bubbled, waving jubilantly.

Though Kim and Jason had been sucking on Verbada's apple sours, they still could not seem to rise to the level of appreciation that Verbada obviously had for her ugly ornaments or her Widgmudgified towns, villages, and cities. The WidgWare ornaments—or 'holiday medallions' as Verbada preferred to call them—looked vaguely like play dough that kindergartners had molded with oily hands prior to its being placed in a can where it would harden and become unusable. The dirty ornaments were misshapen and possessed none of the elegance or charm of other ornaments the children remembered hanging on past Christmas trees.

The *Baby Lonnie* drifted past many more towns, villages, and cities virtually the same as the others they had already seen. One could scarcely glance at any spot without seeing the eyesores that were Verbada's holiday medallions. Just then, Kim and Jason witnessed a scene very different from what they had seen up to this point. A choir, dressed in beautiful and colorful shining Christmas apparel, was singing a lovely carol.

"Are those Orna folk?" Jason asked Verbada.

"Goodness, no!" Verbada lied. "Remember how I told you in my 'once upon a no time story' that there are no such thing as Orna folk?"

"They are beautiful, whatever they are," Kim remarked.

"Don't let their appearance fool you," Verbada stated. "Do you see the ridiculous colors they are wearing? There can be little doubt that they've come directly from some outrageously ridiculous fashion show."

"But their Christmas music is wonderful!" exclaimed Kim.

A look of horror shot from Verbada's eyes. "Obviously, you have been infected with bad music in your past," she said. "What could they be singing? I can hardly make it out."

"I know," said Jason. "Deck the halls with boughs of holly, fa-la-la-la-la-la-la-la-la."

"Don't tell me you like the music, too!" Verbada said with a glint of disapproval in her eyes.

"It's okay," replied Jason.

"Then I was right," remarked Verbada. "You *have* been infected. Deck the halls, boughs of holly, fa-la-la, fa-la-la— what does any of that nonsense mean?"

"Doesn't it refer to decorating the rooms of your house with holly branches?" asked Kim.

"Holly isn't WidgWare, my dear," Verbada stated gruffly, accompanied by a harsh stare. "Who would want to decorate the inside of their houses with clippings from a bush with leaves that stick you? In no time those leaves will dry up, fall off, and clog up your vacuum cleaner. Not only that, but insects hitchhike into your home on those branches and set up housekeeping in your bedcovers. Pretty soon you're not only infected with a ridiculous enthusiasm for stupid leaves that stick you, but your house is infested with spiders, and you've got to call the exterminator. And whatever does fa-la-la mean? It is drivel if ever I heard it!"

The children, who could see no reason to doubt Verbada's criticism of the choir, just stared at her.

"All right, Jason. How good are you at hitting a bull's eye?" Verbada asked.

"Pretty good, I guess."

"Then I'll let you practice target shooting at that choir with my special ray gun."

"Won't that hurt them?" asked Kim.

"Heavens, no, girl," Verbada replied. "It's like an anesthetic that dulls the senses. It will only cause them to change their tune, and that will be all for the best. It may even cure their bad taste in fashion." Verbada called to one of the sailors. "Dinwoody, fetch my secler ray."

"As Queen Lady wishes," he replied.

"Is that the gun you mentioned?" asked Jason.

"Yes, my dear," said Queen Lady, "and I'm going to teach you how to use it."

In a few moments Sailor Dinwoody returned with an odd-looking ray gun. It had a long, clear tube for a barrel and a green handle with a trigger. Coiling down the entire length of the barrel was a spring that seemed to have fish scales engraved on it.

"What is it called again?" asked Kim.

"A secler ray," Verbada replied. She then aimed it at the choir and pulled the trigger, but nothing happened. "Sailor Dinwoody!" she screamed, thrusting the gun at his chest, "How many times have I told you, *don't* bring me my secler ray without first loading it with R.A.A.P.!"

"My apologies, Queen Lady," he bowed. He took out a powder horn, removed a cap from the handle of the gun, poured a dirty, sulfur-colored powder into it, and again handed the gun to Verbada."

"Next time, don't forget," she warned him, and he slunk away.

"What is *rap*?" Jason asked.

Verbada aimed the secler ray at the choir and pulled the trigger. "I'll tell you later," she said. The moment she pulled the trigger, a greenish-yellow laser shot from the barrel, bombarding the choir. "That should do the trick," she said.

Kim looked worried. "What did you just do to them?"

"They needed a good dose of R.A.A.P.," Verbada replied. "It was in their best interest. Just listen."

"What is *rap*?" asked Jason.

"You're much too inquisitive," Verbada replied sharply. "Now listen to the choir like I told you."

The choir was now singing to the tune of 'Deck the Halls', "Flock the boughs with vats of Widgmud, folly, folly, folly, folly la."

"That's more like it," remarked Verbada, snapping her fingers and dancing. "But there is still a problem. Can you tell what it is?"

"No," said Kim.

"Their song is still *too* melodious. Here Jason," she said, handing him the secler ray. "You try shooting them."

Jason took aim. When the ray hit the choir, they stopped singing the melody and started shouting the words in monotone.

"That beat is still *too* rhythmic," said Verbada. "Go ahead and shoot them again," she told Jason.

After they were shot this time, only the rhyme could be heard.

"That sounds like rap music now," Kim noticed. "Is that why they call the powder *rap*?"

"Certainly not," said Verbada. "Rap music still has *too* much rhyme to be tolerable. I'm so glad you noticed the problem," and she took the gun from Jason and let the choir have it with one long laser burst from the secler ray. When she had finished, the music had lost every trace of melody, harmony, rhythm, and rhyme and had morphed into a hodgepodge of senseless noise. "That is much better than before," she finally said. "In fact, it is some of the best Widgmus music my secler ray has produced thus far. Don't you children think it sounds glorious?"

"I guess so," replied Kim.

"You guess so?" exclaimed Verbada. "You *guess* so?" Verbada removed the wrapper from another apple sour and handed it to Kim. "Here, young lady, suck on this and listen more closely. Remember that good music grows on you over time. We'll have to work on your musical taste."

As Kim sucked on the apple sour and listened, she began to appreciate the music more and more, but she also felt like she was being hypnotized. "I think I see what you mean," she said. "The music is as clear as. . .as clear as. . ."

"As clear as WIDG*MUD*?" Verbada interrupted with a smile.

"Yeah, that's it!" replied Kim.

"Now, young man," she said, turning to Jason. "See those lamps along the river?"

"They look like the angel stars you described in your 'once upon a no time' story," he remarked.

"Then they couldn't very well be angel stars, could they?" she stated.

"I suppose not," he answered.

"I'll tell you what you can do to them. Just think of them as opportunities to get our helpful message about WidgWare out to the public," said Verbada. "If you shoot them with my secler ray, they will be instantaneously turned into WidgoVision viewing screens for our infomercials. Believe me. You will be doing them a favor. Feel free to shoot as many as you like."

"Cool," said Jason. He began to shoot the lamps that were 'not angel stars' with Verbada's secler ray until they started glowing with an eerie mixture of green, orange, and dirty pink. "This is really cool," said Jason, as he kept shooting, but the secler ray had soon run out of R.Λ.Λ.P. Realizing that it needed to be reloaded, Verbada shouted to Sailor Dinwoody, "Can't you see the child needs more R.A.A.P. for the ray?"

"At once, Queen Lady, but perhaps I should warn your Ladyship that we are running low," he replied.

"Then we shall have to put in to port," she said. "I'll let the Widgmudgeons know to expect us at the nearest factory."

After Sailor Dinwoody reloaded the secler ray with R.A.A.P., Jason continued to flock the lamps along the river with "vats of Widgmud." Meanwhile, Verbada went to her cabin, put on her cyberbonnet, and sent the Widgmudgeons her communiqués through her thoughts.

—Chapter Five—

THE ONE WHO SENDS SNOW

THE *BABY LONNIE* DOCKED, but no Widgmudgeons as yet had shown up to meet them.

"Where are the urchins?" Verbada yelled. "They have disobeyed me for the last time. They will have to be punished severely for not being here with the shipment of R.A.A.P. Dinwoody, go this minute and find those Widgmudgeons. Bring back the R.A.A.P. shipment from my factory, and be quick about it. Those Widgmudgeons have delayed our plans. As soon as I get back to my cabin, I'm going to use my cyberbonnet to give those little creatures a taste of my displeasure."

"May we go with Sailor Dinwoody?" asked Jason.

"I don't think it's wise for you to go without me," she said.

"Can't you go with us?"

"Absolutely not," Verbada stated flatly. "I never leave the ship except to go to my WidgoVision studio."

What the children did not yet know was that there were reasons why she could never leave the waters of Tinsel Canal.

"I promise we'll be good," Jason begged. Please let us go with Sailor Dinwoody!"

"I'm not sure that's a good idea. Remember the problem you had before with the Widgmudgeons?"

"But I thought you were going to punish them with your cyberbonnet," said Kim.

"True," Verbada said. "Very well, I will let you children go on one condition. Whatever you do, you must not talk to a Widgmudgeon. If one asks you a question, just say, Queen Lady will give you the answer to that. That should shut them right up."

The children agreed and followed Sailor Dinwoody off the ship onto the dock. In no time at all, they were walking through a forest. Snow that had fallen the previous day was now melting and dripping onto their heads.

"A catastrophic snow!" Sailor Dinwoody wheezed with alarm. "We must hurry!"

The children sprinted to keep up. When they arrived at the Widgmudgeon factory, this time there was no sound of whirring engines or stamping machines. Widgmudgeons were nowhere to be found. Just then Sailor Dinwoody let out a blood-curdling scream, his eyes staring in horror at the ground. Beneath the snow were melting bodies of Widgmudgeons! "Queen Lady will be outraged!" he screeched. "The enemy has stopped R.A.A.P. production with snow!"

"What enemy?" Kim inquired.

"You will have to ask Queen Lady that question," said Sailor Dinwoody. "I am not allowed to speak of him. We must return at once to the ship and warn her. She will have to create more Widgmudgeons for sure. She will be furious! Furious!" Sailor Dinwoody sped down the path toward Tinsel Canal with the children trailing him.

Upon reaching Tinsel Canal, they boarded the *Baby Lonnie*. A breathless Sailor Dinwoody rushed at once to Verbada's cabin to break the news to her. When she heard it, she screamed at the top of her lungs. "HOW DARE HE SEND SNOW!" Veins popped from her neck, forehead, and temples like purple snakes trying to eat their way through a layer of pink frog skin. Then her pupils sharpened to a hateful point, and, almost with a whisper, she said through clenched teeth, "How *dare* he send snow!" The very way she uttered the word 'dare' gave Kim and Jason goose flesh.

Verbada stomped up the stairs, shouting orders left and right. "Alert the sludge dredgers! Round up the pie masters! I will show the enemy that I will not be stopped by a little snow!"

Sailors ran off the ship into a nearby town and soon returned with a crowd of beautiful, shining people in shackles and chains. They were dressed like the choir they had seen earlier.

Verbada loaded her secler ray, pointed it at the crowd, and pulled the trigger. When the ray hit them, the shining people turned into not-so-jolly zombies. Their hair became straggly, and their clothes turned to gray and brown rags. Verbada's sailors, looking more like prisoners than prison guards, then released them from their shackles. Some, carrying barrels, began walking out into the river. Others, remaining on the shore, stared blankly at the ground.

"What did you do to them?" asked Kim.

"I need mud for my pies," Verbada answered. "The best mud is from a place called Mud Flats, but we have no time to go there. The mud will have to be dredged. I gave them a temporary case of Widgworms to get them to help me."

"That sounds awful," remarked Jason.

"Oh, don't be silly," she said. "Most of them will recover in time. At worse, they will end up with a case of residual Lesnititus."

"What's that?" asked Kim.

"Never mind!" she answered in a perturbed voice. "You children ask too many questions. You had best not interfere. The situation is critical, and you are pestering me. Here," she said, handing them each an apple sour, "suck on these."

Because Verbada now was frightening them, Kim and Jason pretended to put the apple sours in their mouths, but they in fact threw them into Tinsel Canal while Verbada wasn't looking. They watched as the poor zombies dredged hands full of mud from the bottom of the canal and loaded it in barrels. In a steady stream, they carried the barrels to shore while others began making strange mud pies."

"Sailor Dinwoody," Verbada ordered. "Fetch my cyberbonnet!"

He ran below and a short time later returned with it. When Verbada put it on, it began to turn a putrid orange with splotches of slime green, fungus yellow, and mold gray. Then something startling happened that the children had not seen before. Green laser webs spun out from the bonnet's holes, and pink electrical spiders crawled across them into the mud pies. As the spiders crawled, they made electrical sounds like the dots and dashes in Morse code. Kim and Jason watched in fearful amazement as the mud pies were transformed into Widgmudgeons before their very eyes.

"They're alive," giggled Sailor Dinwoody with a crazed look in his eyes.

The Widgmudgeons seemed even uglier than the ones the children had seen earlier. Some looked so disgusting Kim and Jason could hardly bear to look.

"I know what you're thinking," said Verbada. "Their appearance makes me slightly ill, too. But they are essential for R.A.A.P. production." Verbada's psychedelic cyberbonnet again started changing colors and spinning out green webs. More pink electrical spiders crawled from the bonnet into the heads of the newly created Widgmudgeons. "Your wish is our command," they uttered in one accord. Then they turned and walked away into the forest. Kim and Jason could hear them repeating the words. "We widg you a mudgy

Widgmus, we widg you a mudgy Widgmus, we widg you a mudgy Widgmus, and a wormy WidgWare."

"This incident has delayed us," said Verbada, "but I suppose it can't be helped. At least by tomorrow, there will be enough R.A.A.P. for us to continue on."

"We still don't know what *rap* is," Jason said, hoping to squeeze an answer out of Verbada.

"Some things are best kept secret," she replied. "All you need to know for now is that without R.A.A.P. we could not produce our fine line of WidgWare. And without WidgWare, we could not control Widgmus World, and we could not celebrate Widgmus. Sadly, some lands in our world are still without WidgWare, and the inhabitants of those lands know nothing of Widgmus. The enemy is working overtime to keep WidgWare and Widgmus out. The enemy is against all free trade."

"Is he the one who sent the snow?" asked Jason.

"Ridiculous, isn't it?" replied Verbada. "He rides an ugly mule and wears a crown made out of weeds. His spies lurk about everywhere. You must be careful to steer clear of them because they have been known to kidnap children and to try to brainwash them. You saw what he did to my Widg-mudgeons. He dissolved the poor little things. Heaven knows what he might do to you if you were unfortunate enough to be kidnapped!"

"Now," Verbada said, changing the subject. "It is time that you children got some rest. We have a busy day ahead, and you will need your strength. We will set sail early tomorrow morning."

Verbada led them to a room with two beds and told them another quick 'once upon a no time story'. "Now to sleep with you," she said. "I will see you children bright and early."

After she had left, Kim asked Jason, "Don't you think she is sort of scary?"

"Yes, but she's sort of nice, too," said Jason.

"She wasn't very nice to those zombies or Widgmudgeons," said Kim.

"I guess not," said Jason. "But she did let me play with her secler ray. That was so cool." He pretended to shoot at objects in the room.

"Shhh!" cautioned Kim. "She might hear you. Maybe we should just do as she asked and go to sleep. Good night, Jason."

He pretended again to shoot objects in the room.

"I said, good night, Jason."

"Oh, all right!" He lay down and kept shooting his imaginary secler ray at the ceiling without making noise. Soon he tired of it, and he and Kim went to sleep.

—Chapter Six—

A "VERY-BADDA" HAIR DAY

WHEN DAWN BROKE, Sailor Dinwoody woke the children and commanded them to join Verbada on deck for breakfast. After they dressed in some goofy sailor clothes Verbada had laid out for them, they climbed above board and saw a table set with plates and utensils. Sitting on a platter were shiny gray gooey globs that were oozing a yellowish-orange colored liquid. They looked vaguely like pig brains. Soon Verbada joined them. "I've taken the liberty of making you a delicious breakfast," she said. "I hope you like apple dumplings."

Jason stared at the globs, and they seemed to pulsate. "Could I have cereal instead, please?"

"Cereal!" she cackled. "Young man, I will have you know that these steamed apple Widgmus dumplings were featured on my famous Verbada Cooking show that airs daily throughout Widgmus World! One of these dumplings alone sells for one-hundred widget-wampum! Most people would give their eye teeth to have one! Now try it. I'm sure you will just love it."

Jason and Kim each carefully lifted an apple dumpling from the platter onto their plates like surgeons removing internal organs. As Jason stared at the heap of gray matter, a lump the size of a golf ball formed in his esophagus. Kim tried to take a bite, but it was pasty and sour and did not at all agree with her.

"You don't like them?" Verbada inquired with a raised voice. "What is wrong with you children? Didn't your mother ever serve you a decent breakfast? Very well, if it's cereal you want, then cereal you'll get. Sailor Dinwoody!" she cried. He was not on deck, so she screamed at the top of her lungs, "DINWOODY!" He soon came running.

"Yes, Queen Lady," he answered, cowering.

"These children want cereal." Something about the way she said the word let the children know she was very displeased. After she left the deck, Dinwoody went to get the children their cereal. Upon returning, he served them bowls of soggy gray mush.

"Don't you have crispy cereal?" asked Jason.

"No," replied Dinwoody flatly.

The children, who were hungry, tried to swallow the cereal, but it had the flavor of sour wallpaper paste. Kim could have sworn that Dinwoody had just put the apple dumplings into a blender and pureed them.

In time Verbada returned. "I've just spoken to Captain Rushport. We shall be arriving soon at our WidgoVision studios where our programs are produced. Sailor Dinwoody will give you passes so that you can get in to see the *Dagmus and Baloonia Show*. Meanwhile, I will let Jason entertain himself by shooting more of the things along the shore that are "not" angel stars with my secler ray. He'll be doing me a great service by helping me spread WidgoVision to every town and hamlet of Widgmus World. Kim, you come with me. I need you to help me dress and put on my makeup for my infomercial-take."

Verbada handed Jason her secler ray, and Kim followed Verbada to her suite. When they arrived, Verbada went to a closet, stood on tiptoes, and pulled down a hat box from a top shelf.

"What's in the box?" Kim inquired.

"I call her my Susie Q," replied Verbada, taking it over to her sofa and opening it. Inside was a beautiful Christmas wreath with twelve candles.

"Susie Q looks like the Christmas crown that the 'Lady' person wore in your 'once upon a no time' story," remarked Kim as Verbada removed it from the box.

"You're so perceptive, my dear," said Verbada. Then she looked straight into Kim's eyes. "Now, my sweet, you've heard of make-believe, haven't you? Well, I call make-believe 'Reality Show,'" she said. "In this way, I'll convince the WidgoVision viewers that I am really the Lady person in my 'once upon a no time' story whom I told you never existed."

"Why would you want to do that?" asked Kim.

"Well," said Verbada in a whisper. "There are still some folks in Widgmus World who like to think the 'once upon a no time' story about Lady is true! So at this time of year, when they celebrate whatever it is they celebrate, I wear Susie Q to fool them. You've heard of April Fools' Day of course. The joke will be on them, and they'll never know it. I'll just put on this ridiculous headdress, light the candles, and strut around on a stage singing some of my new Widgmus tunes. I know I look like a coalmincr in it, blinding people with all that light, but they seem to enjoy seeing me in it, nonetheless."

Verbada removed Susie Q from the box and placed it on her head.

"She looks lovely on you," said Kim.

"If you say so," remarked Verbada rolling her eyes. "I shall need to see if the candles will light properly. I always have a problem with Susie Q's candles. They will never light for me, so I'll need your help. I'll just sit here and let you light them for me. Here are some matches."

"I'm not supposed to play with matches," said Kim.

"Oh, don't be silly," said Verbada. "I'll be here to make sure your little fingers don't get scorched. Now be a peach and light the silly candles."

Kim struck the match and managed to light about three of Susie Q's candles before the match had burned down to her fingers and she had to blow it out.

"You're doing just fine," said Verbada. "Just take your time."

Kim struck another match and managed to light another four.

"Very good," Verbada remarked. "One more match should do the trick. We don't want to waste them. If the enemy shows up again, we may need them to set fires to melt his awful snow."

Kim struck the match, but this time, before she was able to light the last candle, the flame got a little too close to her fingers and she accidentally dropped the match right in the middle of Verbada's orange, fried-dyed hair, setting it ablaze. Verbada jumped up with a screech, grabbing a hairbrush and patting out the fire. But several of the candles fell over and ignited her hair again. Screaming at the top of her lungs, she finally managed to extinguish the flame. By now wax had melted into what were five tufts of orange hair sticking up from her blackened scalp. "What have you done to my beautiful hair!" she screeched.

Kim was almost in tears. "I'm sorry. I didn't mean to."

"You didn't mean to!" shouted Verbada. "Just look what you've done!" In a tantrum, she threw Susie Q to the floor. She would have stomped up and down on it, but she knew better than to destroy it. She steadily regained her composure.

"Maybe you could wear your cyberbonnet instead," Kim suggested.

"What?" she cried. "Are you out of your mind? I can't do that! The people I'm selling my WidgWare to know nothing about my cyberbonnet, and you had better not tell them about it either. Is that clear?"

"I promise I won't say anything," said Kim. "I really am so sorry about your hair."

"Oh, stop apologizing, will you?" she grumbled. "Run up and tell Sailor Dinwoody that I shall need him to send for Harrietta Hairnetta, my stylist right away. And please hurry! My infomercial shot is in less than two hours."

Verbada glared at her reflection in the mirror, and dabbed the tears from her cheeks with a tissue; Kim ran and found Sailor Dinwoody. Soon he came rushing down below with Kim and Jason following. "Queen Lady! Oh, Your Ladyship! What happened?"

"Oooo," Jason said to Kim. "Did you do that?"

Kim frowned and slapped him on the arm.

"It's just an accident," Verbada said. "Now, Dinwoody, take the speed boat. Fetch Harrietta Hairnetta and bring her here as quickly as possible. She's the only one who can possibly get us through this crisis. You children must go with Dinwoody. I need to get you out of my hair—and I mean that in more ways than one. You can spend the afternoon in town. Just don't talk to strangers and don't get into any trouble. Do you hear?"

From Verbada's quarters Jason and Kim followed Sailor Dinwoody down into the hull of the river cruiser. He led them to a large bay where several speedboats were waiting. Dinwoody commanded some of the sailors dressed in their jailbird uniforms to mount one of the speedboats onto a launcher.

"Get in," Dinwoody told Jason and Kim, "and put on these life-vests."

Kim and Jason obeyed.

"Now sit down and hold on," he ordered. Then he commanded one of the sailors, "Launch!" and immediately they went sailing through the air.

"Wee!" Jason and Kim shouted. When the boat hit the water, they sped out across Tinsel Canal. The wake left by the speedboat looked like a cross between tarnished copper and yellow sludge. Soon buildings started coming into view.

"Is that the studio?" asked Kim.

"Yes," Dinwoody stated abruptly. After they had docked, Dinwoody told them, "I must go now to find Ms. Hairnetta. Queen Lady said that you may be on your own for a bit. But remember to behave, and try not to talk to strangers."

"Okay," the children agreed.

"Remember, you must be at the studios before the taping of the *Dagmus and Baloonia Show*," he told them. "Taping will begin at 2:00 p.m. sharp, so be there at least thirty minutes early so you can find a good seat, all right?" He reached in his pocket. "Here is some money for lunch." He gave each of them five widget-wampum.

"Thanks," they replied, looking at the strange coinage. It had Queen Verbada's face stamped on one side and the Latin words *reductio ad absurdum* printed around the circumference. On the opposite side was stamped the *Baby Lonnie* surrounded by what seemed to be seven dragon heads.

"I'll see you in a couple of hours then, and don't be late," he said as he departed.

As Kim and Jason walked in the direction of a large, dark clock tower, the clock struck twelve. The bell was so loud, and sounded so harsh, that Kim and Jason had to plug their ears. The tower had a spooky appearance, like the tower of a haunted mansion. It had a four-sided steep roof, flat on top, with ornate black wrought-ironwork around its perimeter. Dark gray lines of shingles cascaded down each of the four sides which were separated by more of the ornate ironwork.

When the horrible bell ceased ringing, very odd-looking characters began flooding the streets.

"Look," said Jason. "It's the balloon people and toothpick trees we made! They're here, but look how big they are!"

"You're right," Kim said. "I hope Mom had a chance to snip the sharp points off the toothpicks."

"They still look pretty sharp to me," said Jason.

"Yeah, they do," said Kim. "Let's just hope they don't get too close to one another."

Vendors quickly set up stands in the streets and placed signs that read "Windbaggits" and "Needlenoggins." The

Windbaggit stands had what appeared to be large soda-pop tanks, while the stands of the Needlenoggins had tables with dozens of cartons like the ones from a Chinese takeaway. Soon lines began to form in front of the signs, and it became clear that the balloon-headed people were the Windbaggits, while the wooden-headed ones with porcupine quills were the Needlenoggins.

As the lines formed, angry shouting filled the street. Kim and Jason noticed that the Needlenoggins would shout at the Windbaggits and chase them until the Windbaggits would pucker up their lips, which incidentally looked like the open end of a balloon, and would let out a gale that would cause the Needlenoggins to blow over on the pavement. This happened several times until they heard a loud "pop!"

"This is not good," said Kim. "Mother did not fix the problem."

"Now would be a very good time for armor," Jason commented.

Shouts of "Murder! Murder!" erupted from a group of Windbaggits. It seemed a Needlenoggin had sneaked up behind a Windbaggit and burst its head with a mere touch of his finger. Soon a crowd of Windbaggits had surrounded the guilty Needlenoggin and exhaled hot air until every needle was blown off him and he looked like a plucked chicken. "To prison with the pinhead!" they bellowed, and a few moments later the street filled up with police that looked vaguely like the zombies the children had seen earlier. The police arrested the Needlenoggin and carved "guilty" with a knife into his bare wooden skin. As the Needlenoggin was dragged away, he loudly protested, "Hare-brain air-brains! I'll call my lawyer! Then you'll see who stands and who pops!"

Kim and Jason simply stared at each other in shock. They watched as things settled down and lines began to form again in front of the stands. The vendors were shouting, "come and get your grub here!"

"Maybe we had better get something to eat before the lines get too long," Kim remarked, and soon they were standing in one of the lines.

—Chapter Seven—

THE *DAGMUS*
AND BALOONIA SHOW

KIM AND JASON FILED in behind the Windbaggits simply because they looked less threatening than the Needlenoggins, covered as they were with their sharp toothpicks.

"I do feel sorry for that poor pinhead, excuse me, Needlenoggin. Forgive me for being so impolite," Kim and Jason overheard one Windbaggit saying to another. "Who knows, he may just be a victim of his narrow Needlenoggin upbringing. I'm sure he cannot help being the way he is."

"Point well taken," replied the other Windbaggit. "I don't understand why they can't be freethinkers like us. Why do they always have to nail down everything? I would hate to be a butterfly in one of their gardens."

Kim and Jason gave each other a puzzled look.

"Oooo, that is a scary thought," the first one replied. "Just imagine how it would feel to have a stake driven right through your heart as though you were a vampire!"

"I'm sure most Needlenoggins think that anything that flies is a vampire," the second replied. "They absolutely despise anything having to do with air as you well know."

Soon, Kim and Jason had reached the front of the line and noticed that the tanks which they thought contained soda pop were in fact filled with helium. After one of the Windbaggits got hooked up to the tube and took a long deep breath, he burped and then sighed, "Ah, delicious." Then the second Windbaggit got pumped up with gas and made the comment, "Wow, I'm stuffed. That's one of the best breaths of fresh air I've had in a long time."

Kim and Jason gave each other a strange look and immediately decided to get out of the Windbaggit line before they too got pumped full of gas. They decided to join the Needlenoggin line instead. The Needlenoggins, however, were angry, grumpy, and seething at the injustice suffered by the Needlenoggin who had just gotten arrested for popping the head of a Windbaggit.

"Well, what can you expect of people who have clouds for brains," one of them said to another who was in line behind him.

"And fuzzy clouds for brains at that, without a streak of lightning for common sense," the other remarked, causing the Needlenoggin just ahead of him to laugh and to slap his knee.

"I would love right now to prick their puffed up heads till their brains popped out. I would do it for sure if I knew they wouldn't blow their air-brained ideas in my face and stink up the atmosphere with them. How great it would be just to pop their heads and watch their dreams fade into the surrounding atmosphere without having to smell their foul breath as they drone on and on!"

The other Needlenoggin kept erupting in laughter, which seemed only to encourage his companion to continue his tirade. "Of course," the first Needlenoggin continued, "it would be our luck to get caught up in their sticky thoughts like an insect in a spider's web. Most likely, even the clearest and cleanest thinking Needlenoggin would die struggling to escape the maze of Windbaggit bamboozlement."

The children continued to watch the Needlenoggins as they sneered and threw the evil eye at the Windbaggits, but the Windbaggits seemed oblivious. Soon the children reached the front of the line and discovered that the white pasteboard cartons were filled not with food but with nails, tacks, thorns, and cactus stickers, "the kind of stuff you can really sink your teeth into," they had heard one Needlenoggin remark with delight.

Jason and Kim realized that there was no normal food to be found in the town, and having had no breakfast, they were growing very hungry. In fact, they were so hungry that now even Verbada's grayish apple dumplings seemed appetizing. Suddenly, the bell from the clock tower sounded, and they saw that the hands were pointing to a quarter after one. They were afraid they might be late for their meeting with Sailor Dinwoody, so they hurried back in the direction of Widgo-Vision studios.

They arrived amid pomp and circumstance to shouts of "Queen Lady!" A large crowd had gathered at the dock, waving and cheering, as Verbada Widgmud, sitting on an orange and pink throne, arrived from *Baby Lonnie* by a longboat rowed by Widgmudeons. When they docked at WidgoVision studios, her servants lifted up her throne on staves while she continued to wave royally to the crowds.

Kim and Jason felt proud that they knew such an important dignitary so well, and they tried to break through to see her. Sailor Dinwoody, however, found them first. "I have front row seats for the *Dagmus and Baloonia Show*. Hurry and follow me."

They trailed Sailor Dinwoody into the studio, and the first thing they noticed was that its floors were made of transparent glass. Through it they could see the sinister waters of Tinsel Canal flowing beneath.

"Queen Lady will not be sitting with you," said Dinwoody, guiding them to their seats. "She will see you following the show."

Kim and Jason noticed that the upholstery of the seats was of orange and pink vinyl, and when they sat down, it felt sticky and uncomfortable. The studio audience was also gathering. Oddly, the Windbaggits migrated to one side, and the Needlenoggins, to the other. When two o'clock approached, the studio darkened and they heard a voice announce over the loud speaker, "Now, coming to you live, from WidgoVision Studios! It's *Dagmus and Baloonia!*" The spotlights brightened, revealing a well-dressed Windbaggit woman and a well-groomed Needlenoggin man sitting in armchairs, smiling and waving. "Featuring our hosts Dagmus Trench!" the announcer continued as the Needlenoggin man waved, causing half the audience to boo and the other half to cheer. "And Baloonia Bologna!" As the Windbaggit woman waved, the booing and the cheering from the audience were reversed from the way they were before.

"Brought to you by WidgWare!" continued the announcer, bringing immediate applause from the entire audience. This was the only thing they enthusiastically agreed upon.

"Today, on *Dagmus and Baloonia*," the announcer spoke again. "Is it really more blessed to give than to receive?" A picture of a boy suddenly flashed on the screen. "Find out what this young man is teaching his parents about gifts for the holiday season." Then a picture of a girl flashed on the screen. "And—this Windbaggit girl would rather pop than live with her Needlenoggin parents. Would you like to know why? And finally—taking the elf threat seriously. What can be done to stop the elves from spreading their lies about Widgmus? All of this, coming to you live on *Dagmus and Baloonia*, so stay tuned. But first, a word from our sponsor."

The applause died down, and singers broke in with "and a jingle, jingle, jingle all the way" as the spotlight revealed Verbada wearing a red wig and the Susie Q. She danced and sang to the tune of "Jingle Bells," "'WidgWare sales,

WidgeWare sales, WidgWare holidays. With WidgWare on your Widgmus Tree, you will never have to decorate again.' Hello, I'm Verbada Widgmud, creator of fine WidgWare products for holiday décor." Various odd-looking WidgWare decorations flashed on the screen. "Are you tired of holiday ornaments that break easily or become tarnished over time?"

As Verbada spoke, Jason looked through the glass floor and noticed that something was happening to the waters of Tinsel Canal flowing beneath. The dark part of the waters turned slime green, and the golden streaks became shaped like pink and orange horseshoes. He shook Kim and whispered for her to look.

Kim stared at what Jason saw, and Verbada continued her commercial. "Let us show you our fine line of durable and colorful WidgWare for your Widgmus Tree. Your children will dearly love a WidgWare Tree this Widgmus,"

The horseshoe shaped streaks now started joining together, making the waters of Tinsel Canal look like snakeskin. Kim and Jason stared at one another, wondering what this could mean.

"So come and visit one of our fine stores soon," Verbada went on, "where all WidgWare is always on sale." After these words, she again broke into her 'WidgWare Sales' song. When she had finished, the lights turned up again on the talk show hosts.

"Welcome to today's *Dagmus and Baloonia Show*," said Baloonia. "First on our show: Is it really more blessed to give than to receive? We have as our guest today, Charlie, who has been challenging this conventional holiday wisdom." The image of the boy that flashed on the screen earlier was shown again. "Charlie, welcome to *Dagmus and Baloonia.*"

"Charlie, is it true that your parents tried to get you to give them gifts by brainwashing you?" asked Baloonia.

"Yeah."

"Can you tell our audience what your parents tried to do to you?"

"Yeah," he said. "They kept telling me stupid stuff over and over. At first I didn't know what they meant."

"What did they tell you, Charlie?" asked Baloonia.

"They kept telling me that 'it is more blessed to give than to receive.' I ended up giving 'em back my allowance and working for 'em for nothing. They really took advantage of me."

The audience gasped.

Baloonia made a serious face, "Okay," she said somberly. So you reported your parents to child welfare. Can you tell us what happened next?"

"Yeah," Charlie replied. "My mom and dad got fined big time for teaching me their wrong ideas. They really got taught a lesson."

Dagmus chimed in. "Tell me, Charlie. Have your parents learned their lesson?"

"I guess so," he said. "But they haven't paid my allowance, so I'm going to have to take them to court again."

"Why haven't they paid you?" asked Dagmus.

"They claim the fines took all their money," Charlie answered. "So they think they have an excuse not to pay me my allowance. But they still expect me to work."

"That is terrible," Baloonia interrupted. "Your parents are very unjust."

"I disagree," Dagmus spouted. "The only mistake the parents made was to teach the boy that it is better to give than to receive. If they had taught him the opposite, Charlie wouldn't have a leg to stand on."

"I don't understand how you can say that," Baloonia returned. "It was their choice as parents to have a child in the first place. He didn't ask to be brought into the world. If you ask me, the parents are to blame not only for bringing Charlie into the world, but for making him feel guilty for not doing something that was totally their idea."

"Well, Charlie," said Dagmus. "I just wish we could drum some sense into your parents' heads and help them realize that it's more blessed to receive than to give. If they had taught you that, then you wouldn't have gotten all mixed up."

"Your opinion again," returned Baloonia, "so it's time for our audience to decide who's right. We'll have the verdict after this message from our sponsor."

The lights faded and the "jingle, jingle, jingle" music again introduced Verbada. "Do you want to cut down on holiday expenses but give the best gift possible during this jolly season?" she asked. "Then your answer is WidgWare."

Jason and Kim again saw the snakeskin pattern form under them in Tinsel Canal. The terrifying sight of it caused them to draw their feet up onto their seats.

Verbada's WidgWare pictures again flashed on the screen. The zombie faces of the audience now reflected the snakeskin ripples of Tinsel Canal below.

"And don't forget," continued Verbada. "WidgWare is as durable as it is attractive. No Widgmus Tree can be complete without it. So come and view our excellent line of WidgWare holiday medallions at your nearest WidgWare store. And remember, all WidgWare is cheap and fashionable, and the wonderful WidgWare colors will fill the eyes of your children with delight and joy."

When she had finished, the audience broke into riotous applause, but Kim and Jason merely frowned at each other. They could not understand why the only thing the audience could agree on was Verbada's WidgWare, especially considering how ugly it was. The lights again were turned up on Dagmus and Baloonia.

"As usual, we have let the audience decide who is right, and as usual, the vote is evenly split." Suddenly the children heard several pops. It seems that some of the Needlenoggins in the audience had popped the heads of several Windbaggits. This was followed by a gale which sent pine needles sailing off some of the Needlenoggins through the studio.

"Ouch," Jason cried. "One of those needles hit me right in the head."

Kim examined his forehead and found a spot of blood. "It doesn't look too bad," she assured him.

Meanwhile, security and medical emergency teams rushed into the audience and carried away a group of quarrelling Windbaggits and Needlenoggins. "Take those Needlenoggins to court and sue them!" shouted some of the Windbaggits.

"We're lucky to have such lively participation in our audience today," Dagmus laughed.

"Yes," said Baloonia, "and thanks for staying tuned. Now for the next topic on our show." The picture of the Windbaggit girl shown earlier again flashed on the screen. "This is Wendy. She says that she would rather pop than to continue living with her Needlenoggin parents. I wonder what the audience thinks about that?"

Angry shouts came from the Needlenoggin section of the audience, while the Windbaggit section stood, cheered, and gave Wendy a standing ovation.

"It appears that our audience is evenly divided on the topic as usual," said Baloonia.

Dagmus spoke up. "Wendy, Dagmus here. What exactly is the beef that you have with your parents?"

"My parents enjoy making me keep stupid rules," replied Wendy. "They just want me to be miserable. I've tried to get them to see that every one of their rules is crazy," replied Wendy, "but they are too set in their ways to bend an inch."

"I'm sure your parents are just trying to get you ready to fit into society and be a good citizen," said Dagmus.

"The *Needlenoggin* version of society, Dagmus?" Baloonia probed. "The *Needlenoggin* version?"

"Of course," said Dagmus. "Is there any other version that makes sense?"

The Needlenoggins in the audience applauded, but the Windbaggits booed.

"Can I say something?" asked Wendy. "How does sleeping with my head pointed east rather than west help me to fit into society? That's a stupid rule if ever there was one. My parents just have control issues."

This time, the Needlenoggins booed, and the Windbaggits applauded, shouting, "Right! Right!"

Baloonia frowned. "Surely, Dagmus, you have to agree with Wendy here. Her situation illustrates so well why rules are made to be broken."

Again the Needlenoggins booed, and the Windbaggits clapped.

"It is clear, Baloonia," returned Dagmus, "that you believe in only one rule."

"Yes, Dagmus, and what rule is that?"

"The rule that every rule is made to be broken."

"You are trying to be clever, Dagmus," said Baloonia. "But it won't work. You are just playing mind games with the audience."

"How is that possible with your supporters?" asked Dagmus. "In the first place, games have rules, and your Windbaggit bunch doesn't believe in rules. How can anyone play mind games with them? In the second place, how is it possible for someone who has an airbag for a head to have a mind?"

"Your insults only reveal your own close-mindedness and stupidity, Dagmus," Baloonia returned. "If anything, you and your breed have daggers for minds. You don't care the least bit that this wonderful child, Wendy, would rather pop than put up with torture from her cruel Needlenoggin parents. You have no sympathy whatsoever."

"I have sympathy for anyone who has to listen to Windbaggits like you drone on and on and on."

As Dagmus and Baloonia argued, rumblings kept coming from the audience, back and forth from Windbaggits to the Needlenoggins, back again to the Windbaggits, and then to the Needlenoggins. In time, the rumblings of the audience reached a fevered pitch, and they seemed on the brink of rioting.

"I think the audience will have something to say about this," said Baloonia. "As usual, we'll let them decide. The verdict when we return. Now another message from our WidgWare sponsor."

The spotlight came up on Verbada, who was sitting by a fireplace. "Hello there, friends," she said in a mellow voice. "During this happy season, we all want to spread the joy of Widgmus to our friends and neighbors, especially those who don't share in the Widgmus spirit."

Kim and Jason again stared at the waters of Tinsel Canal beneath the glass floor. This time, when the snakeskin appeared, they thought they also could see a serpent's head rising from the water. They drew their feet up onto their seats again.

Verbada stood and held up a WidgWare ornament. "Wouldn't you just love to spread Widgmus cheer to everyone you know by giving them the gift of WidgWare this holiday?"

The faces of the audience again basked in the eerie light coming from Tinsel Canal as Verbada continued her sales pitch. "You have your choice of an assortment of colors, and don't forget, WidgWare is so durable, you can be sure that it will grace the Widgmus trees of you and your friends for many years to come. As you purchase your fine WidgWare products, just remember (and she sang softly) 'with WidgWare on your Widgmus tree, you will never want to decorate again'. Now, back to the wonderful hosts of our show, Dagmus and Baloonia."

"We have again let the audience decide," said Dagmus. "This time, Baloonia, I hate to say that your Windbaggits have been outvoted by one vote!"

The Needlenoggins cheered, but the minute they did, the Windbaggits released another gale of hot air. Then the Needlenoggins retaliated. Pops were heard throughout the audience, followed by bursts of air. Again, the security and medical teams came to the rescue, carting off the wounded, and arresting the rioters. The audience now was roughly one-third of what it had been at the beginning of the show. When a semblance of order had been restored, Dagmus came on.

"Finally on our program this afternoon," he said, "'taking the elf threat seriously.' Baloonia, what do you think should be done?"

"Well, Dagmus," said Baloonia. "As you know, there is a rumor that elves have been threatening Widgmus World ever since someone called 'Lady' was allegedly imprisoned in a place the elves call Black Tower."

"That is interesting, Baloonia," said Dagmus. "Why does this pose a problem for Widgmus World?"

"Well," said Baloonia, "they claim that Widgmus World is really a place called Arboria, but the most controversial allegation is the claim that their 'Lady' is the real Queen Lady, and that she is being held hostage by kidnappers from Widgmus World!"

"If that were true, it would be unfortunate," said Dagmus.

"Of course," replied Baloonia. "But the claim of the elves is clearly unsubstantiated. The truth is that this old woman went into self-imposed exile."

"Why did she go into exile, Baloonia? Do you know?"

"The rumor among the Needlenoggins is that she was old, sick, tired, and fed up with the state of affairs in Widgmus World," said Baloonia, "but that can hardly be right."

"There you go, Baloonia," Dagmus asserted. "I should have figured that those words would come from your mouth. Why not just tell the truth. If she did go into self-imposed exile, she most likely was sick of all your hare-brain air-brains with their wacky way-out ideas."

"I hardly think that could be true, Dagmus," Baloonia challenged. "More likely than not, she had had all she could take of hardheaded, hardhearted Needlenoggins like your-self. I'm sure she got tired of your prickly crowd trying to 'pin her down' on every issue."

"Are you sure it's not your airbag horde who has alienated the elves and incited them to spread their lies to all good citizens of Widgmus World?" asked Dagmus.

"I would hardly call them lies," returned Baloonia. "That's the way all your Needlenoggin friends think, isn't it? If someone expresses the least difference of opinion, you call it a lie."

"Surely you're not defending the elves' claims," challenged Dagmus. "They need to learn to accept Widgmus World as it is, just as all decent citizens must do."

"There you go again," said Baloonia. "And whose version of Widgmus World are you referring to? The version of your pinheads?"

"Better that than a world where every halfway decent idea gets blown away by hot air from your windbag brigade."

"Maybe we just misunderstand what the elves want from us," said Baloonia. "Maybe they are just freedom fighters struggling for their independence. Shouldn't we show some sympathy with their cause?"

"Sympathy with their cause!" shouted Dagmus. "Their cause is to bring back Christmas, and you know what that means! Widgmus World and the WidgWare Empire will crumble!"

"Well, I wholly disagree," said Baloonia. "I believe you are exaggerating the elf threat."

"I don't believe you are saying that," Dagmus returned. "The elves hate us and want to destroy the economy of Widgmus World."

"I figured that for your kind it would come down to money," said Baloonia. "You fat cat Needlenoggins are forever worried about your pocketbooks. If you ask me, you need to open up your bank accounts and support the elf charities."

"You mean support elf revolutionaries?"

"I would hardly call them revolutionaries," replied Baloonia. "In your world, everyone has to think exactly like you. Can't people just live and let live?"

"Or die, and let die?" said Dagmus. "Would you propose we do nothing about the threat of an elf revolution?"

"There is no such threat," stated Baloonia flatly. "The threat is all in your mind and the minds of your fellow Needlenoggins."

"At least we have minds!" Dagmus returned. "Don't you understand that the elves want us dead?"

"Surely you exaggerate," Baloonia responded. "Even if they did want to see us dead, which I don't believe they do, it would only be because there are too many of your Needlenoggin kind getting them riled up. If you would just let them be who they want to be, they would have no reason to hate us."

"You are wrong, Baloonia!" stated Dagmus. "Wrong! Wrong! Wrong!"

"Well, I think there is no doubt in our minds about your opinions, Dagmus," replied Baloonia. "As usual, we'll let the audience decide. We'll hear from them in a moment after a public service announcement from Verbada Widgmud."

Again, Verbada appeared on stage, dancing and singing 'with a jingle, jingle, jingle all the way'. This time, her WidgWare commercial featured little poor children being interviewed by her public relations manager.

"Hello," said the interviewer. "My name is Quirinius Grousenot. . ."

"Grousenot," Jason whispered to Kim. "Isn't that the person Verbada was talking to over the telephone?"

"Yes, shhhh," Kim returned.

Grousenot continued, ". . .the Widgmus Children's Fund is a non-profit organization run by WidgWare Enterprises to help the poor orphans of Widgmus World have a fighting chance. Just ten widget-wampum can help rescue a child from dire poverty." A picture of a little boy with a very dirty face flashed before them. "Will you be a Scrooge this Widgmus? Or will you help a little Tiny Tim like this child have his Widgmus turkey and eggnog?"

"That boy looks familiar," whispered Kim.

Then a picture of a girl holding a box of matches flashed on the screen. "And for a contribution of twenty widget-wampum, you can help this little match girl buy matches to light her very poor family's Widgmus candles," Grousenot went on.

Kim whispered to Jason. "Hey, that's my face. And the boy's face was yours, Jason. Somebody took our pictures and doctored them!"

Just then, a harsh reprimand of "shhhh!" came from behind, and the children became quiet.

"And with a contribution of one-hundred widget-wampum," continued Quirinius Grousenot, "you can help literally hundreds of children in Widgmus World have a very special Widgmus. Please make your donations to the Widgmus Children's Fund, care of Verbada Widgmud Enterprises, *Baby Lonnie*, Tinsel Canal. That's the Widgmus Children's Fund, care of Verbada Widgmud Enterprises, *Baby Lonnie*, Tinsel Canal."

Verbada Widgmud reappeared. "And I promise that WidgWare Enterprises will match your gift, widget-wampum for widget-wampum. So dig deep into your pockets now and give all you can."

Again the entire audience clapped for her, and Kim and Jason could see both Needlenoggins and Windbaggits taking out their checkbooks and wallets to give money to the charity. The children noticed that the audience had now dwindled due to the many casualties and arrests that had taken place.

Dagmus and Baloonia returned to close the show.

"We're back," said Baloonia. "As usual, we have agreed to let the audience decide."

Again the vote of the audience was taken. Again the vote was equally divided. Again heads of Windbaggits popped and needles were blown off the Needlenoggins. Again security and medical emergency came, leading equal numbers of Windbaggits and Needlenoggins away. Another vote was taken, and again the vote was tied. Realizing that the show was almost over, the audience started rioting, and they battled one another until there were no Windbaggits or Needlenoggins left except Dagmus Trench and Baloonia Bologna.

After the show, as Dagmus and Baloonia were preparing to exit the studio, Verbada came onto the stage and congratulated them for their great performance. "Truly, it is more blessed to receive than to give," she joked as she gave

Dagmus and Baloonia two large buckets full of widget-wampum. "Here's your cut," she said. "Thanks to those children my Widgmudgeons captured, we have raked in a tidy sum tonight for the 'Widgmus Children's Fund.'"

Dagmus and Baloonia laughed.

"You've put on a good show tonight," Verbada told them. "The money will go a long way toward putting new carpet in my boardroom."

"You are the 'fairest of them all,'" Baloonia complimented her, "and in more ways than one."

Verbada straightened her headdress with the twelve candles and smiled.

"I never thought I would agree with Ms. Bologna," Dagmus added. "But you are the Queen of Widgmus World and the best example of how it is more blessed to receive than to give." Verbada thanked them again and began to walk away, forgetting Kim and Jason. The children soon caught up to her.

"Oh, it's you," she said sharply. "I'm sorry I don't have time for you now. I've an appointment to keep."

"But we're hungry," said Jason.

"Well, now. You should have thought of that earlier when I offered you the very delicious and filling apple dumplings," replied Verbada. "Those would have stayed with you all day. But you children made your choice, didn't you? You'll just have to be hungry and wait." With these words she walked away slamming the studio door behind her.

—Chapter Eight—

CAPTURED

WHEN THE CHILDREN left the studio, the clock on the tower pointed to three o'clock, and the streets were now abandoned. They wandered in search of something to eat and eventually came to the edge of town.

"We had better not go this way," said Kim. "There's nothing but forest."

"I'm so hungry," Jason said. "Can we go in just a little ways and maybe search for nuts and berries?"

"Don't forget what happened when we went into the forest before," Kim reminded him. "We might be captured by Widgmudgeons again; or worse, we might cross paths with the enemy Verbada warned us about—the one who sends snow."

"But I'm starved," Jason said, wincing, "and there's nothing to eat back in town."

"Okay," said Kim. "But don't say I didn't warn you. Let's just stay close to the road in case we have to run back for safety."

Jason and Kim ventured into the forest and started searching the thicket.

"Hey, look!" exclaimed Jason, stooping down, "a walnut. Look, here are some more."

He handed several of the nuts to Kim, and she squeezed two of them together until they cracked. "Ouch, that hurts." She tried to pick out the meat. "It's no use," she complained. "We'll starve this way. I wish we had something to pick the meat out with."

Kim and Jason kept trying to pick the meat out with their fingers, but the shells were thick and very hard, and there was very little meat inside.

"I give up," said Jason, throwing his walnuts at a tree. "Let's see what else we can find."

They traveled further into the wood, but before they knew it, they had fallen into a large hole. They got up and tried to climb out, but the hole was too deep, and its sides, too steep to scale.

"What now?" asked Jason.

"Shhh," Kim gestured. "Do you hear that?"

They listened.

"Widgmudgeons?" Jason whispered.

Kim shushed him again.

Then yank! Their feet flew out from under them. They were caught in a net. The next thing they knew, they were being pulled up. They screamed for help. They heard chattering. It got louder and louder, filling them with dread. As they were pulled out of the hole, they saw creatures with pointed ears.

"Space aliens!" shouted Jason.

"Don't be silly," Kim corrected him. "They're elves. Can't you see?"

"Remember what Dagmus Trench said?" Jason whispered. "Maybe we've fallen into the hands of elf kidnappers."

Kim's face turned pale.

One elf, who wore a crown, was obviously their king. He began interrogating them. "Are you spies?"

"No," Jason blurted.

"What business do you have here?"

"We were looking for food," said Kim.

"Why here?" stated the Elf King.

"We couldn't find anything to eat in the town but air, nails, and stickers," said Jason.

"Town?" remarked the Elf King.

The Elf King's minister whispered into his ear, "They must be on the side of the enemy."

"We're not," said Kim, overhearing. "We know who the enemy is. Queen Lady told us. He's the one who sends the snows that melted her Widgmudgeons."

The elves' eyes filled with horror and their faces turned quite serious as they again started murmuring amongst themselves.

"Silence," ordered their king. "They are only children. They do not yet know the difference between right and wrong. She has gotten to them."

"Could they have eaten forbidden fruit?" the minister questioned.

"We haven't eaten any fruit!" Kim exclaimed. "We only ate a few nuts. We promise that we didn't eat your fruit."

"Now we know they cannot be trusted," said the minister. "If they have been near the enemy, there is a chance they have already eaten."

"I fear you are right," the Elf King agreed.

"Eaten what?" asked Kim.

"Do you crave the forbidden fruit?" asked the Elf King. "If you have eaten it, you will only want more. It causes terrible hunger."

Kim felt the hunger gnawing at her stomach. "I don't remember eating any fruit," she said.

"The enemy has other tricks," said the minister. "Remember her cooking shows? She has found so many ways to disguise her poison."

Jason and Kim turned pale and gave each other a fearful look.

"Have you eaten any of Queen Lady's food?" the Elf King asked.

"Only her apple sours and some of her apple dumplings," said Kim with a terrified look.

The elves gasped.

"Then you have been poisoned, I'm sorry to say," said the Elf King. "What else did she give you to eat?"

"Only the apple sours and apple dumplings," said Kim. "I don't believe they were poisonous," she stated flatly.

"If they had an apple flavor, then they were poisonous," said the Elf King.

"I knew something was wrong with her food," Jason whispered to Kim.

"Be quiet," Kim told Jason.

"Don't you remember how awful those apple sours tasted when we first put them in our mouths?" Jason repeated.

"I don't believe he is telling us the truth," Kim whispered to Jason. Then she questioned the Elf King. "We are still alive, aren't we? If we had been poisoned, wouldn't we be dead by now?"

"The poison is slow acting," the Elf King told her. "You must believe that I am telling you the truth. The good news is that there is a cure. There is only one problem. Anyone who has fallen under the full spell of Verbada's poison usually does not want to be cured."

"Can we be cured?" asked Jason.

"Jason," Kim whispered to him. "You can't trust him. How do you know he is not making up a story?"

"It depends," the Elf King replied to Jason. "Did you start enjoying her apple sours after a while?"

"I guess so," said Jason.

"That is a bad sign," the Elf King told him. "It could also explain why you are so hungry. Do you know how Verbada brews her flavoring for her apple sours and apple dumplings?"

They shook their heads.

"She concocts it from something called R.A.A.P. Have you heard of it?"

Jason's eyes widened. "Yes," he replied with a nervous wiggle in his voice. "That's the powder she uses to make her secler ray work."

"You know of that awful weapon?" the Elf King inquired.

Jason gulped. "Yeah, she let me shoot things with it."

The elves gasped again, mumbled among themselves, and shook their heads. Jason's face turned pale with fear.

"Do you know how R.A.A.P. is made?" he asked.

"From sludge dredged from the bottom of Tinsel Canal." Jason wrinkled his nose in disgust. Then it dawned on him. "You mean the apple sours we ate were made from sludge? Gross!"

"I don't think he's telling the truth," Kim said to Jason.

"Indeed," the Elf King said to Jason. "Now just answer one question. Are you hungry enough now to eat one of Verbada's apple dumplings and enjoy it?"

The children stared at him and said nothing. They realized they would have to answer "yes" to his question.

"It is as I feared," said the Elf King, reading their thoughts. "You are feeling the effects of the hunger that her poison brings on—the hunger that ever grows. But your hearts and minds also may have been affected more than you know. Are you still confused about who the enemy is? If you believe I'm telling you the truth, would you be willing to give your life defending it?"

At that moment, a dark shadow passed over Kim's face, and her pupils shriveled to a point. "No," she replied. She knew deep inside that something foreign had taken over her mind and voice, but she felt powerless to fight it. "We know who the enemy is," she continued. Her voice sounded cold and harsh. "He is the one who rides the mule and wears the crown of weeds—the one who sends the snow."

"You see," the Elf King said to his men. "Their minds have been ensnared by her charms. It may be too late to help them. We shall see."

"Children," he said sternly. "We shall try to convince you through reasoned arguments that the enemy is not the one who sends snow. This one whom you call the enemy is in fact our king, the Lord of Arboria. You must now come with us. We will do our best to break the spell Verbada has put on you and deliver your minds from her curse."

"No," Kim shouted. "We don't want to go. Jason, help me fight them! They will use his snow to melt us. We saw what he did to the Widgmudgeons!"

Obeying his older sister, Jason began to struggle and kick.

"Bind them," the Elf King commanded his men. The children screamed and fought to get loose from their ropes, but the elves knew how to tie the tightest of knots. Soon the elves were leading Kim and Jason in procession through the forest.

"You'll be sorry!" Kim shouted. "Queen Lady has a cyberbonnet. She will send her electrical spiders to bite you. She will zap you with her secler ray."

The elves sadly shook their heads at Kim's words and continued to lead the children deeper into the forest. In time, they came to a place where snow had freshly fallen. The children became extremely frightened.

"Are they taking us to the enemy?" Jason asked Kim.

"Don't worry," she whispered to him. "We'll figure out a way to escape."

Eventually, the elves led them to a grove of enormous trees that resembled a fortress.

"They will have to be locked up for a time," the Elf King told his men. "They are hungry. Offer them snow bread and see if they will eat it. If they will not, I don't know what we can do to help them. Their hearts may have already turned to mud."

The elves locked the children up in a cell that was not nearly as nice as their room on Verbada's boat. After the elves had left, Jason began to cry. "What are we going to do? What if our hearts have turned to mud as he says? If we eat the snow bread will our hearts melt?"

"Don't believe anything he says," said Kim. "I have a plan. They are on the side of the enemy Verbada warned us about for sure. I'll try to make them think we have seen the light and that we now believe that Verbada is the enemy. After we get them to trust us, we'll make a run for it."

A little while later, an elf maiden arrived carrying a basket of bread. "Children, I know you must be very hungry. This bread is for you. It is snow bread made from the pure snow sent by the King of Arboria, the Keeper of the Forest whose home is at Tree Top. It will satisfy your hunger no matter how terrible."

The children's eyes became filled with terror. "We're not that hungry anymore," Kim lied. "Can't you just please let us go? We are not your enemy."

"I cannot let you go without the Elf King's permission. Meanwhile, be of good courage and let this sweet snow bread sooth your hunger."

When the elf maiden left, she locked the cell, and Kim and Jason stared in horror at the basket of snow bread.

"We can't be sure that this isn't the real poison," Kim said to Jason. "Quick! Stuff it into your pockets. When the elves return, I'll try to convince them we ate it."

They both hid the bread in their pockets. In time the elf maiden returned to see if they had eaten, "how was the snow bread?" she asked.

"Good," both of the children fibbed.

"Now will you let us go?" asked Kim.

"You will have to talk with the Elf King," the maiden replied. "I shall summon him."

She left, and about an hour passed. By now Kim and Jason were starving. But something inside them made them resist eating the snow bread at all costs. Suddenly they heard shouting and the sound of warfare echoed from the elf camp. A guard ran and opened the door to their cell. "You children must run for your lives," he said panting. "The enemy has found us, and you are no longer safe here. Flee! But whatever you do, do not go back in the direction of the town. You must run deeper into the forest and hide there until the fighting is over. Then you must search for the land of the orphan children until you find it. That is the only safe haven now."

When Jason and Kim left their cell, they saw a horrible sight. Widgmudgeons were fighting the elves with dark swords that flashed green, orange, and pink. "Run for your life," Kim told Jason, and soon the children were scurrying into the forest. They hadn't gotten far, however, when they were jerked up by someone's hands. "Help! Widgmudgeons!" shouted Jason, but then he noticed that it was Sailor Dinwoody who had found them.

"You children should have known better than to wander into the forest," he scolded. "Are you mad? Do you not realize that the elves are fighting on the side of the enemy? The enemy's snow is like acid. You're lucky he didn't melt you with it as he did the Widgmudgeons we saw earlier."

"We tried to tell Queen Lady we were hungry," said Kim, "but she just ignored us. She told us she had to go to an important meeting. We were just looking for something to eat when we got lost."

"Remember how Queen Lady tried to get you to eat her delicious apple dumplings when we were on the *Baby Lonnie*?" Dinwoody remarked. "Maybe in the future you will do as you're told and eat your apple dumplings without making a fuss."

While they walked, the children noticed Sailor Dinwoody was leading them back in the direction of the town. "The elves said the enemy has taken over the town and warned us not to go there," she blurted.

"Not *your* enemy, you silly girl," replied Dinwoody, "*their* enemy. Have you let them brainwash you? Rest assured Queen Lady has everything under control. You now have no reason to be afraid."

When they reached the Tinsel Canal, they climbed back into the speed boat that had brought them to WidgoVision Studios. When they arrived back at the *Baby Lonnie*, the boat was hoisted back up into the bay that it was launched from earlier. "Queen Lady will want to see you," Dinwoody told them. "She is liable to be quite angry with you for disappearing."

"Will she punish us?" asked Jason.

"She will give you a good talking to, that's for sure," he replied. "She will make sure the elves haven't corrupted your minds with their ridiculous lies. It is very important that you not believe anything they told you."

When the children arrived at Queen Lady's parlor, they noticed that she was wearing her cyberbonnet. The green laser webs were spinning furiously from it in great numbers, and thousands of pink electrical spiders crawled along them sounding like electrical Morse code. She was deep in concentration when the children entered. "Stop right there!" she told them, "and don't say a word! I have very important matters to tend to! I will deal with you in a minute!"

Kim and Jason stood as still as statues, watching Verbada as she worked. Her face at one point became dark and wrinkled.

"Turn away!" she ordered. "I don't appreciate your watching me like that!"

Kim and Jason obeyed, but they could still hear the shrill sound of the green laser webs spinning from her cyberbonnet. The crackling of the pink electrical spiders as they ran down the webs made chills run down their spines, and not being able to see Verbada's face filled them with even greater fear.

Finally, the squealing and crackling stopped, and Verbada spoke. "I'm sorry you children had to see that, but it's your fault I had to take care of that nasty business. Don't you children realize the danger you put us all in? You fell into the hands of elves! The very thought of it makes me bristle! There is no telling what would have happened to you if I hadn't come to your rescue."

"We didn't realize they were so dangerous," said Kim.

"Well I hope you know now what serious trouble you were in," replied Verbada. "You're lucky they didn't turn you into frogs! You might even have become a slave to Old Red Coat!"

"Who is Old Red Coat?" asked Jason.

"He's one of the enemy's admirals," she replied. "You don't want to know what he does to children. He brainwashes them so that they will fight for the enemy's cause. They become part of what we call the Orphan Brigade. You can't imagine what would have happened to you if we hadn't saved your hides."

"Now," she said, changing the subject. "I've had to make my Widgmudgeons use valuable time cleaning up the mess you created by consorting with the elves. Because you've stirred up this mess, the enemy may try to retaliate. The enemy's chief aid, Old Red Coat, has a dangerous battle ship. He may very well try to engage us here on Tinsel Canal. I hope you children feel very sorry for all the trouble you've caused me."

"We are," said Kim. "We were just hungry and wandered into the forest to find food."

"I'm sure you didn't find much food there either, did you?" she replied. "I suppose now you will be grateful for one of my apple dumplings, won't you?"

Kim and Jason hung their heads.

"WON'T YOU?" Verbada shouted.

"Yes, ma'am," they said, quivering.

"Or, perhaps you would you rather go hungry?" she said, reading their faces.

"No," said Kim. "We're starving. One of your apple dumplings will be fine."

"Very well," said Verbada. "DINWOODY!" she screeched. He soon appeared at the door. "Serve up plenty of apple dumplings to the children! They are now ready to learn how to appreciate fine dining aboard the *Baby Lonnie!*"

—Chapter Nine—

POISONED

SAILOR DINWOODY LED a reluctant Kim and Jason from Verbada's cyberbonnet control center onto the deck where a table was set. Engraved in the middle of the plates was Verbada's lightning trademark that they had seen so many times before.

"Sit," Dinwoody commanded.

They obeyed, and he went to prepare their apple dumplings.

"Have you noticed that Queen Lady is acting strangely?" asked Kim. "Why did she make us look the other way when she used her cyberbonnet?"

"I don't trust her anymore," Jason remarked. "Could the Elf King be right about her apple sours and apple dumplings? Remember how terrible they tasted at first?"

"You're right about that," replied Kim. "But what if the elves really are kidnappers and revolutionaries? Can we believe what they told us? Remember what Dagmus Trench said?"

"Yeah," Jason returned, "but Baloonia Bologna said that there is no threat of elf revolution. There's another thing I can't figure out. Why did Dagmus and Baloonia argue with each other but not with Queen Lady? And why did Queen Lady use our faces to talk about the Widgmus Children's Fund? I think she was just using those doctored pictures of us to get more widget-wampum for herself."

"What was that she said about the Orphan Brigade?" Kim remembered. "Maybe the money was for them?"

"I don't think so," said Jason. "Remember what the elf said who let us go when the Widgmudgeons attacked? He told us not to return to town but to run into the forest and try to find the land of the orphan children. Don't you see? They are Queen Lady's enemy? So they must be on the side of the elves and 'he who sends snow.'"

"Quiet," Kim cautioned. "Sailor Dinwoody is returning."

Dinwoody slopped the apple dumplings on the plates in front of them and said in a gruff voice, "Eat. Maybe now you'll appreciate Queen Lady's exquisite apple dumplings. She expects you to eat every bite of them."

Sailor Dinwoody watched them as they stuck their spoons into the gooey gray mass. Jason's and Kim's hunger was terrible, but the stench of the apple dumplings made their stomachs turn. They remembered it well. It was the smell of the bubbles in the Tinsel Canal, the smell of rotten eggs mingled with apple cider vinegar.

"I told you to eat!" shouted Dinwoody. "Do it, or Queen Lady will have to punish you!"

The children crammed a spoonful of the apple dumplings in their mouths, and gagged. The horrible stinking globule refused to slide down their throats.

"Queen Lady is going to be very ANGRY!" Dinwoody's tone was cruel and scary. "It looks as though she will have to start you back on apple sours to get you to the apple dumpling stage again. Do you see what trouble you've caused? Your time with the elves has reversed your progress. You've fouled up Queen Lady's wonderful plans for you. She is extremely busy now, but you've made it necessary for me to go inform her that you are not eating her delicious food." With these words Sailor Dinwoody stormed away.

Once he had left, Jason blurted, "Verbada is trying to control us with her apple sours and apple dumplings just as she controls Widgmudgeons with her cyberbonnet!" At that split second, he reached into his pocket, pulled out the snow bread the elf maiden had given him, and devoured it.

Kim's eyes bulged and almost popped out of their sockets. "Jason, are you crazy?"

Jason clutched his chest and fell to the ground as though he had been wounded.

Kim ran to his aid. "Jason! Jason! You've been poisoned!"

About that time Verbada emerged on deck with Sailor Dinwoody following close behind. "What's all this commotion?" Her eyes fell on Jason who was still lying on the floor. "What's the matter with him?"

"He's been poisoned!" Kim shouted hysterically.

Shock flashed across Verbada's face. "How dare you say he was poisoned by my wonderful apple dumplings!"

"Not by your dumplings," Kim cried. "He ate the elves' snow bread!"

The pupils of Verbada's eyes sharpened to a point. "Snow bread!" she said with a tone of horror. "DID THE ELVES GIVE YOU SNOW BREAD?" she screamed.

"Yes," replied Kim, pulling hers out of her pocket.

"Ye gads!" Verbada uttered, placing her hand on her forehead as though she were going to faint. She fanned herself. "Dinwoody! Get the disposal bin for hazardous waste!" Then she ordered Kim. "Put that down, child. It is deadly! Deadly!"

Kim placed her snow bread on the table, and Verbada's face radiated horror. "Oh no, now it's touched the table! The table will have to be destroyed!"

She pulled out a flask of her apple cider vinegar. "Put out your hands," she ordered Kim. Kim did as she asked, and Verbada liberally doused them with the vinegar. "Now rub vigorously!" she commanded, and Kim obeyed.

By now, Kim was weeping. "What about my brother?" she asked.

"The snow bread will melt his heart," Verbada stated coldly. "He most likely will not survive its spell. Even if he lives, he likely will be hopelessly confused for the remainder of his life."

"No! Please, no!" Kim cried. She bent over with the intention of embracing Jason, but Verbada yanked her back.

"What are you doing? Remember what I said about having to destroy the table because the snow bread touched it? Your brother has been contaminated."

"You can't destroy him!" Kim cried back. "He's a person!"

"We won't destroy him, silly girl," Verbada informed her. "We will just have to have him quarantined until we can manage to send him off to the land of the orphans."

"The land of the orphans!" Kim exclaimed. "Then I may never see him again."

"You will learn to live without him in time," Verbada reassured her. "Just be glad you are not an orphan yourself. In fact, I've got a wonderful idea. Why don't you let me officially adopt you as my daughter? I promise to take good care of you. And just think. When the time comes for me to retire, you will inherit my WidgWare fortune. As my daughter, you will be the heiress of Widgmus World and the immense wealth of WidgWare enterprises! Believe me when I tell you it will be better this way. Even if your brother should survive poisoning by snow bread, you wouldn't want to waste your life taking care of an individual who has lost his wits. You would be miserable. Don't you see that this is all for the best?" Verbada put her arm around Kim, and pulled her away from Jason. "Now come with me, and we'll make wonderful plans for the future, you and I. You'll see."

As they walked away, Jason regained his senses and sat up. "I'm as free as a bird," he shouted.

Verbada stared at him. "What?"

Jason stood up and placed his hands on his heart. "I'm free. And you are uglier than I ever remember! Let go of my sister, you old witch."

Kim just stared at him.

"You tried to turn our hearts to Widgmud," Jason accused Queen Lady. "Well it might have worked for a little while, but then I ate the snow bread. The snow bread melted the Widgmud away. Now I can see what you're up to."

"It's as I feared," said Verbada with a hint of pity in her voice. "He has become hopelessly lost."

Kim started weeping.

"She's lying, Kim. Don't believe her," Jason pleaded.

"Now you won't be able to believe a word he says," Queen Lady said to Kim. Then she shouted, "Dinwoody!" and in a few moments he appeared. "Be sure the men use gloves. He may be contagious."

Dinwoody left and soon returned with some sailors dressed like jail birds. "Take him below," Dinwoody ordered.

"No," Kim wept, trying to break loose of Verbada's grip.

"It's no use, child," Verbada told her. "You can do nothing for him now. He must be removed from the ship, or the virus he's caught from the snow bread may infect us all." Kim could not control her sobs. "Now, now," said Verbada, trying to comfort her. "Come with me, and we will have fun together eating apple sours and telling 'once upon a no time' stories. I will help you forget about your brother."

Verbada put her arm around Kim's shoulders, and led her below. Kim was sad and quiet. Her thoughts were with Jason, and she could hardly believe that he had been so stupid as to eat the snow bread.

"Don't worry, my dear," said Verbada. "I know you are tired and need to be alone for a time. I'll leave you now to go to bed. Things will look brighter in the morning, you'll see."

Kim went to the room where she and Jason had slept during their first night on the *Baby Lonnie*. She tried to sleep, but she couldn't stop thinking about Jason. Several hours had passed when she decided to go up on the deck and get some air. While she was standing there, she heard a roar. Then she saw a motor boat flying out from the launch, and in the boat were Dinwoody, Jason, and a couple of sailors.

"Jason!" Kim shouted to him, and he turned to look at her.

"Kim!" he shouted back. "Just try to think of Verbada and her Widgmus World as a 'once upon a no time' story. Try to hang on! I promise I'll be back to rescue you!"

Kim waved a last goodbye and returned below to her bed. She finally fell asleep, but her dreams were troubled with visions of Widgmudgeons fighting elves, and of Verbada's cyberbonnet spinning out green laser webs and breeding thousands of pink electrical spiders. But worst of all, she dreamed that she grew up and became Verbada herself. She dreamed that Jason had made the right choice when he ate the elves' snow bread. The horror of the thought woke her up, but she soon sank back into an uneasy sleep.

—Chapter Ten—

THE ORPHAN BRIGADE

DINWOODY AND HIS henchmen's motor boat sped down Tinsel Canal, and they shot cold and hateful stares at Jason. "Where are you taking me?" he kept asking, but they simply ignored him. The motor's sound grated on Jason's ears, and the rotten sulfuric stench of Tinsel Canal lodged the memory of Verbada's apple dumplings in his brain as they once had in his throat. He wished now that he had more of the elves' snow bread to eat to help him drive the putrid smell from his nose.

"I feel sick to my stomach," Jason informed Dinwoody.

"Shut your trap," he snapped, "or I'll throw you overboard."

Jason repeatedly stifled the urge to vomit. He glared at the waters of Tinsel Canal, and the ripples moved mysteriously into the same snakeskin pattern that had appeared beneath the glass floor of WidgoVision Studios whenever Verbada performed one of her infomercials.

When they had reached the shore, Dinwoody commanded his lackeys, "Dispose of this piece of garbage!" and they obeyed. Grabbing Jason's arms and legs, and gripping them so hard they hurt, the henchmen started heaving him back and forth until they released him. Jason sailed through the air, hitting the bank with a thud. Slowly he pulled himself up and lifted his head only to see the motorboat speeding away. Dinwoody and his men were spewing out coarse laughter, jeering at him, and pointing at him with scorn. Jason, now covered from head to toe with stinking mud, gagged, coughed, and spit. He could only repeat the word "yuck!" over and over as he stood and, without success, tried to wipe the gooey slime from his hands onto his just-as-slimy trousers.

Jason looked about. The shore was deserted. He remembered Kim. She may be able to take care of herself, he thought, but who's going to take care of me? His older sister had always pampered him and come to his rescue when he was in a tight spot. Now he worried that something bad might happen to her—and to him for that matter. He walked away from Tinsel Canal, and kept shouting, "Yoohoo! Anybody there?" If he were lucky, elves might capture him again. Now he would be glad to eat some of their snow bread.

Jason wandered down a path that wound through a maze of thick holly bushes clustered with crimson berries. After he had traveled a little ways, he came to a rough ivy-covered stone wall that appeared to have once belonged to a castle. The ivy leaves had the look and feel of green velvet. "Hello!" he shouted toward the top of the wall. There was only silence. Placing his foot in an indention in the stones, he started climbing. He grunted as he pulled himself up. With his right hand, he grabbed hold of a jagged rock. He found another hold for his left foot. Eventually he swung his left arm onto the top of the wall and pulled himself up. As he did, he cut his chin on one of the stone's sharp edges. Now, lying on his belly at the top of the wall, he caught sight of a snow bank on the other side. Hanging with both hands he eased down and dropped to the ground. He rubbed his chin where he had cut it. A smear of blood mixed with the mud on the back of his hand. Mom would have doused the scratch with alcohol, so he was glad she was not there to make a fuss. He trotted over to the snow, knelt down, and rubbed his hands in it. "Aye, aye, aye, that's c-o-l-d," he said, his teeth clattering. To his amazement, the dirt on his hands disappeared. "Oh, wow!" He took a deep breath, plunged into the snow bank and rolled in it. Shooting to his feet, he jumped up and down and jogged in place to generate heat. The sudden crisp scent of fir trees rushed inside his nostrils. He checked his clothes and hands, and his eyes widened in amazement. No trace of the disgusting mud lingered on him or his clothes. He drew his hands up to his mouth to warm them with his breath. As he did, he sniffed. Wow! His hands were now covered with the heavy scent of freshly cut fir! The scent made him feel alive for the first time since he had come to Widgmus World. Almost instantly, the snow had banished the putrid smell of mud from his mind. He buried his face in a handful of snow, rubbing it on his lacerated chin. When he removed the snow from his face, his eyes focused on a red spot of blood that stained the pure white powder. Then, in a magical instance, the spot of blood turned into a berry like the holly berries he had seen on the bushes. "This is really wild!" he said to himself. He scooped up more of the snow and tried to make another blood imprint. This time, when he removed it from his chin, it contained no bloody imprint but appeared entirely unspotted. He brushed the snow from his hands and felt his chin. The cut was totally gone! "Unbelievable!" he exclaimed. He jumped up and started running through the woods. Whenever he saw another of the snow banks, he would jump in it and roll about. The snow now seemed less chilly than before, and he found that he could easily mold it into shapes. "Gosh, Kim would love this," he said as he started packing snow and sculpting it. Kim had an artistic flair that made Jason jealous. Whenever they played with modeling clay, the objects Kim would make always looked more original and detailed than Jason's. He could tell by his mother's reaction. Mom always bragged on Kim more than she did on him. In fact, Jason wondered why his mom had hung the horrible looking WidgWare ornaments on their Christmas tree since they looked uncannily like some of the ugly clay models he used to mold. As Jason shaped the snow, he wondered if his work of art might turn out to look like one of Verbada's hideous looking Widgmudgeons or like one of her WidgWare ornaments. He sat molding the shape for some time, not noticing at first that he was making something very beautiful and exquisite. Before his very eyes, the snow began to take shape. First, the head of a horse appeared. Jason could hardly believe how perfect it looked. The legs and tail appeared next. Though Jason knew he was doing the sculpting, the shape that was now appearing seemed as though it had been trapped in the snow all along just waiting for him to liberate it from its icy shell. When Jason started working on the back of the horse, a hump appeared that at first made the horse's back look like that of a camel. But as he packed on more and more snow and continued to shape it, a distinct human form began to emerge—and not just any human form—it was the form of some kind of prince, because a crown began to appear on its head as well. Jason now brushed off the last fragments of excess snow so that the legs and feet of the human figure were now as crisp and clear as the horse's features. Once he was finished, he stood to admire his work, hardly believing his eyes that he had produced so perfect a sculpture. But scarcely a minute had passed when he heard neighing. The snow horse reared, and the figure on its back slapped it to make it ride. "Good grief! It's alive!" he exclaimed. The horse jaunted back and forth, moving in tight circles as the face of the human figure remained turned toward Jason. Then to Jason's amazement, the statue he made began to grow until it was full size, and as though the snow had been only a layer of thin powder, it fell off revealing a real white horse ridden by a real prince dressed in a forest green robe lined with white fur. He wore an exquisite crown of holly and ivy.

"You have summoned me," the princely figure stated. "Do you know why?"

Jason, speechless, shook his head.

"No matter. It's best you come with me."

"Who are you?" Jason asked.

"I am Krissmon, Prince of Arboria," he replied. Then he stretched out a muscular arm. "Here, grab hold." Jason latched on, and Krissmon hoisted him onto the back of the horse. "Hold tight," he told Jason. Then he dug his heels into horse's flanks, and they galloped off. Jason held on for dear life. The horse's hooves struck the earth with a steady beat like that of a drum as they swept through the forest's trees. Their reassuring sound made Jason feel secure, safe, and peaceful. In a short time, they reached a clearing, where more holly bushes, dotted with crimson berries, grew. Soon they were entering a field of grass that glittered gold in the sunlight. In the distance were pitched hundreds of forest-green and crimson tents. As they drew closer, Jason could see that the doorways, edges, and corners of the tents were lined with gold brocade covered with all kinds of white symbols, and in the field next to the tent young boys and girls about Jason's age stood in military formation holding muskets. Towering in front of them stood a man dressed in a red-velvet cloak lined with white fur, and on his head was an admiral's hat the same color as the robe, which was also lined with fur. As the man issued commands, the children obeyed.

"Their commander is Admiral Kringle," Krissmon told Jason. Krissmon slowed his steed from a gallop to a trot and finally halted next to where Admiral Kringle stood. Immediately the admiral ordered his forces, and they turned and saluted Krissmon who stretched his hand toward them in a sign of blessing.

"Well done, you children of Arboria's True Queen," he said. "I have urgent news, so listen closely. Our time is growing short, and I promise that each of you will see action before the week is out. There are still recruits to train. This one who rides with me is known as Jason," he said. "He will have good reason to join our cause since his sister is being held captive by the Queen of Mud and is in mortal peril."

A lump formed in Jason's throat.

"It is our good fortune that Jason was not badly injured by the enemy's evil hordes, perhaps because Verbada Widgmud, for whatever reason, took a special interest in him. However, Jason's sister may not be so lucky, and this means that we must succeed in her rescue. Kim's release from her clutches is of the highest importance because she has been brainwashed by their so-called 'Queen Lady'. It is now doubtful that anything short of a forced kidnapping will succeed in freeing her. Her brother may still have some influence over her, so plans for the operation must be made quickly and planned out in careful detail. Then we can turn our attention to more pressing matters. Our first priority is to proceed to Mud Flats and liberate Lady from Black Tower where Verbada has her imprisoned.. This will not be easy because it is heavily guarded by Widgmudgeons and other misshapen zombies she has created out of the riffraff of her decaying, stinking world."

"Admiral Kringle!" the Prince ordered. "Has the *Donna* been readied for the battle of Tinsel Canal?

"It has, your Highness!" he replied.

"Have the elves been thoroughly readied for battle?"

"They have, your Highness!"

"Then Jason and I must now visit the wounded. I want him to see firsthand the dirty work of Verbada's evil Widgmud Empire."

Admiral Kringle saluted again, and Prince Krissmon and Jason rode away. Soon a large white tent came into view. Two guards, dressed in white from head to toe, guarded the entrance. The buttons of the guards' coats were of pure gold, and their white helmets had gold visors. On their coat sleeves were embroidered cross-shaped insignias of intertwined holly and ivy. Gold buckles gleamed on their white shoes. When Prince Krissmon rode into view, the guards stood at attention. After he and Jason dismounted, the guards saluted, and Prince Krissmon reciprocated, following with the words, "At ease."

"Follow me, Jason," Krissmon said, turning to him. "I must show you what terrible things Verbada Widgmud has been doing to the children of Arboria."

Jason followed Krissmon into the tent, and saw row upon row of hospital beds filled with sick and neglected children. Some appeared malnourished. Others had bruises on their faces and arms. Still others wore bandages or casts on their necks, arms, or legs. Virtually all of them were not only bedridden, but were also in various kinds of traction.

"These are the children of the True Queen of our Tree World whom we call Lady. I am her first born," the Prince told him, "so they are my little brothers and sisters."

"I thought Queen Lady was the true queen of Widgmus World," said Jason.

"Most certainly not!" replied Krissmon. "The True Queen of our world is not Verbada, and its name is not Widgmus World, but Arboria," returned Prince Krissmon, who began to move from bed to bed to greet the children. As he did so, he smiled, placed his hand on their heads, and blessed them. "Verbada Widgmud is a usurper and an imposter," Krissmon continued. "Do you know what that means?"

"Not really," Jason replied.

Moving to the next bed, the Prince blessed another child. "It means that Verbada figured out a way to imprison Lady in Black Tower by stealing her Christmas crown and learning how to use its power. Verbada cursed the candles of the crown so that they could never again shine with the true light and meaning of Christmas. However, she decided that she would wear the Christmas crown on special occasions in order to fool the Orna folk of Arboria into thinking that she was the real queen of our Tree World."

"She told us about the Orna folk in one of her 'once upon a no time' stories," Jason remarked.

"Isn't that the most absurd thing you've ever heard?" asked Krissmon. "A 'once upon a no time' story? What good can come from a story like that?"

Jason just shook his head. "I know about the Christmas crown, too," Jason remarked. "Verbada calls it her Susie Q."

"That figures," said Krissmon. "But its real name is not the Susie Q but the Susan, which means 'lily'. Lady's symbols are the lily and the rose, while mine are the holly and the ivy. Stealing the Susan was part of Verbada's diabolical conspiracy to take over Arboria and change its name to Widgmus World. Her real motive was to get rid of Christmas by making the Orna folk believe in Widgmus instead of Christmas. You've seen her secler ray no doubt?"

"Yes," replied Jason. "She let me play with it."

"If you had only known what that horrible weapon was doing to our world, you would never have touched it," said Krissmon sadly. "It erases the true meaning of Christmas from everything it shoots. Verbada literally wants to replace the beauty, glory, and meaning of Christmas with piles of her horrid mud."

"She uses stuff called rap to make her secler ray work," Jason remarked, "but she never would tell me what it is. Do you know?

"How do you think the word is spelled?" Krissmon asked.

"R-a-p?" Jason asked.

"No, it's R.A.A.P.," Krissmon corrected him. "Do you know what those letters stand for?"

"Not really," Jason replied.

"R.A.A.P. is the abbreviation for *Reductio Ad Absurdum* Powder," Krissmon explained. "Those are Latin words meaning 'reduction to absurdity'. Verbada uses R.A.A.P. in her seclar ray to reduce anything having to do with the meaning of Christmas to utter absurdity."

"Now I understand," remarked Jason. "She made me shoot a choir that was singing a Christmas carol while we were sailing down Tinsel Canal. Each time I shot the choir, the music and words to their song sounded more and more absurd. Pretty soon all you could hear was senseless noise."

"I'm glad you've seen through her deception," said Krissmon. "It's sad, however, that so many Orna folk in our Tree World have begun to believe her. Verbada has now almost succeeded in bringing our whole world under her deceitful control. She forbids the Orna folk to refer to the Tree World as Arboria, and she hates the word Christmas with a passion. She will do anything to call it by some other name. Her real aim, of course, is to sell her ugly tree ornaments—her 'holiday medallions' as she calls them. They are nothing like Christmas ornaments, but look like they came straight out of someone's worst Halloween nightmare." Krissmon's eyes looked stern, but they softened as he passed to another bed and blessed the child lying there. Then he asked Jason. "Aren't you the least bit curious about what happened to these poor children?"

"Yes," said Jason.

"They were injured in battle against Verbada. After she imprisoned Lady, these children did everything they could to liberate her. But Verbada's hoards of evil creatures fought them tooth and nail—and I do mean tooth and nail. Widgmudgeons have a nasty bite, if you don't already know that. A scratch from one of their fingernails is so infectious it can cause gangrene."

"Is that why some of the children are bandaged?" Jason asked.

"Yes," Krissmon replied, moving to another bed and blessing the child lying there. "But none here will lose a leg or an arm. This I promise."

Jason watched Prince Krissmon blessing the children. He remembered how Verbada deceived the Needlenoggins and Windbaggits into contributing to the Widgmus Orphans Children's Fund and how she had pocketed the contributions after giving Dagmus Trench and Baloonia Bologna each a cut. Now he realized that she must have been covering up for the horrible things she and her Widgmudgeons had done to these children.

Jason started to worry about his sister. "I'm afraid Kim may end up here, too," he told the Prince. "Will we be able to rescue her in time?"

"Perhaps," said Krissmon. That is why I am here to make these children well. We need more troops if we are going to succeed in fighting her Widgmudgeons. But I am worried about something much more serious regarding your sister than a head or limb injury," Krissmon continued as he moved from bed to bed, extending his hand in blessing. "Kim is in danger of being taught by Verbada to manufacture Widgmudgeons. If she learns Verbada's dark art, there may be little we can do to rescue her. Even now, Verbada is concocting one of her cauldrons of Widgmus eggnog spiked with her powerful apple cider vinegar. It has the most disgusting smell and taste imaginable, but if she can just get Kim to drink enough of it that she begins even remotely to like it, then Kim will become one in spirit and purpose with Verbada. Kim will in fact grow up to be nothing but a younger version of Verbada."

"If her awful eggnog is anything like her apple dumplings, I don't believe Kim will drink any," said Jason. "Verbada made us try her dumplings, but they just made us gag."

"That's a good sign," said the Prince. "But you must realize that Kim refused to eat the elves' snow bread, and that is a bad sign."

"How did you know about that?" Jason inquired.

"I have ways of knowing," Prince Krissmon replied. "Besides, you alone were exiled from the *Baby Lonnie*, right? If Kim had eaten the snow bread, she would have seen through Verbada's stunts just as you did, and she, too, would have been sent into exile. I'm really surprised Verbada's henchmen did not injure you as she did these children. That's her usual way of paying people back for double crossing her. She must have been worried that Kim had enough conscience left to resist her if indeed any harm had come to you. Verbada knows enough to be kind when it suits her larger plans of course, although for her, being kind is quite a difficult effort. Still, I worry that Kim may get hungry enough to eat Verbada's apple dumplings, and no doubt, she will be given a tankard filled with Widgmus eggnog to wash the dumplings down when this happens. She only needs to do this a couple of times before she begins to crave Verbada's poisonous cuisine."

"Poisonous? Will it kill her?"

"It will destroy her ability to care—her ability to show mercy to those who are needy and helpless and sick, such as these children. She will come to the point that if the child lying there were you, Jason, she would be just as coldhearted as Verbada has been toward these children. This is why somebody will most likely have to board the *Baby Lonnie* in order to kidnap her."

"The time is growing short," said Krissmon. "Watch now and you will see a snow miracle." He raised his right hand, and immediately snow began to fall inside the tent!

"You're the one who sends snow!" Jason shouted, feeling a bit perplexed.

"Yes, I am the one who sends snow; the one Verbada calls the enemy."

"But there are no clouds, and the snow is falling inside the tent!" exclaimed Jason, straining to see where the snow was coming from.

"True," Krissmon replied. "But this is not just any kind of snow. This is the snow that washes away Verbada's evil curse. Remember how the snow made the mud disappear from your clothes, and how it made the cut on your chin vanish?"

"Yes. The blood turned into a berry. How did you know that?" asked Jason.

Krissmon pointed to his crown, "This berry right here is yours, Jason." Just then, the children began to get out of their beds and to yank off their bandages. Where there had been wounds, there were now little red berries bouncing on the floor. "Wow!" Jason exclaimed. At that moment, Krissmon began a stirring motion with his right hand, and the berries started swirling up off the floor in keeping with the gesture. With his left hand Krissmon put his palm out toward the berries and then pointed to his crown as if he were beckoning them to join the other berries that were already in it. They swarmed through the air until they came to nest amid the wreath of holly and ivy that graced his head.

"The children's wounds, like your wound, were transformed into holly berries because of a great sacrifice that was made before our Tree World came to be," Krissmon said. "In time you may come to understand the full meaning of this sacrifice."

The children were jumping up and down for joy. They ran up and hugged Prince Krissmon. Then some of the children joined hands and began dancing in a circle around him as little ones ducked in and out of the circle by passing under the joined hands of the others. As the snow grew deeper, Krissmon raised his hand. The snowfall magically halted. The children were already making snowballs and were throwing them at each other. One child about six years old threw one at Krissmon, and it zoomed past his head, barely missing him.

"That's enough," he warned. "Save your enthusiasm for Verbada's Widgmudgeons. Admiral Kringle and the other children are waiting for you. Some you will already know because like you they were injured in the battle against Verbada and were made well. Now go and join them. We must prepare for the battle of Tinsel Canal and embark by morning."

Hugging one another and slapping each other on their backs, the children ran from the tent.

CHAPTER TEN

"Now come with me," Krissmon said to Jason. "We've got to make plenty of snowballs for the ice cannons. Admiral Kringle must set sail by morning."

—Chapter Eleven—

PREPARATIONS FOR WAR

KIM HAD BEEN CRYING for some time in her room on Verbada's palace cruiser. As Jason's older sister, she felt responsible to protect him, and she was now worried sick over what Verbada possibly had done to him. She was angry with Queen Lady for exiling her brother. Verbada had tried several times to cheer Kim. She brought her apple sours and apple dumplings, but Kim refused to eat. Verbada also tried humoring Kim by telling her a funny "once upon a no time story."

"What did you do to Jason?" Kim shouted at Verbada.

"Jason is just fine, sweetheart," Verbada reassured her. "We just thought he needed a bit of therapy after he ate that horrid snow bread the elves force-fed him."

"They didn't force-feed him!" Kim shouted. "He was hungry because he didn't like your horrible apple dumplings."

Verbada bristled but kept her cool. "Well, if he indeed freely chose to eat the snow bread, that is an even worse tragedy," Verbada stated flatly. "Do you want your brother's mind to plummet into madness?"

"No," said Kim, wiping the tears from her eyes.

"Then you've got to trust me," Verbada urged. "Jason is now in good hands" (which was the only thing Verbada had said that was true) "and I'm sure he will soon be much better and will be able to return here healthy and in his right mind. Please don't worry about him. Now," she said, changing the subject, "I've got some wonderful medicine that will help you not to feel so sad." Verbada walked over to the cupboard inside Kim's cabin and pulled out a little tea cup and an amber-colored bottle. Then she poured a tiny bit of liquid from the bottle into the cup and returned with it to Kim. "Here," she said. "Drink this, and you'll feel much better."

Kim lifted the cup to drink, but immediately put the cup down when she got a whiff of its disgusting sour, sulfuric smell.

"It *is* medicine, remember," said Verbada, "and I know it may taste unpleasant at first, so let me sweeten it up for you."

Verbada went to the cupboard again and this time brought back a cup of sugar and a teaspoon. She added several scoops of sugar to the horrendous mixture and stirred it.

"Try it again, my dear," she said. "And if you must, hold your nose as you swallow it."

Kim lifted the cup with one hand, pinching her nose with the other, and sipped. The mixture still tasted very disgusting despite all the added sugar.

"Try to drink it all," said Verbada. "I promise you'll feel better in no time flat."

Kim finished the medicine.

"Now if you will just take a little nap, when you awake I'm sure you'll feel all better."

After Kim drifted to sleep, she began to have very odd dreams. She dreamed about Widgmudgeons, but they no longer seemed hideously ugly to her. She dreamed instead that they were like her cute little pets. They would come up and nuzzle her, making little puppy dog and pussy cat faces, and she would tickle them and pet them. Then they would frolic around her and speak in what she imagined was some kind of baby talk. "You're just precious," she would say, and they would pant and lick her face. She also dreamed that Verbada was her mother, and that no one ever had a more wonderful mother than she. Kim dreamed that they would spend hours talking about their wonderful Widgmus World plans. "You will be my apprentice," Verbada would tell Kim, and Kim would get very excited. Kim also dreamed that Jason had become very mean and that Jason had told her he hated her and never wanted to see her again. She dreamed that Jason made her cry, and that Verbada had urgently run up to her and asked, "My dear, what is the matter?" And Kim had replied, "Jason is an old 'meany.'" Then she dreamed Verbada broke the difficult news that Jason was truly not her child and therefore could not possibly be Kim's brother. "In the goodness of my heart," Verbada had told her, "I adopted the poor orphan. But he was always disobedient and incorrigible. Though I tried and tried to be a good mother, he became impossible to handle, so I finally had to send him away to a school for juvenile delinquents where he could get help. The very thought that I had to do that to the poor little thing makes me extremely sad." Kim dreamed that Verbada then hugged her and kissed her on the forehead with the words, "but you and I, my dear—we will be okay—I'll tell you what I'll do. I'll teach you how to make my special mud pies, and after you've learned how to do that, I'll show you how to create Widgmudgeons! Just think of it! You'll get to wear my cyberbonnet and learn how to control Widgmudgeons with your thoughts! It will be such great fun, you'll see." Kim's dream then began to change, and she dreamed that Verbada had named her Chairman of the Board at WidgWare Enterprises, putting her in charge of the production of the entire line of holiday medallions. She dreamed that at the annual Widgmus party, she was recognized as Apprentice of the Year and was given a plaque that read "In grateful appreciation for services rendered to WidgWare Enterprises." The party was a black-tie affair, and all the notables of Widgmus World were present, including WidgoVision talk-show hosts, Dagmus Trench and Baloonia Bologna. They toasted Kim with mugs of Widgmus eggnog, and when she sipped it, she at once thought, How wonderfully scrumptious this tastes! Mother has outdone herself on this batch! Mother. Yes, it was true. Verbada really was her mother, wasn't she?

Kim awoke to find Verbada hovering over her bed with another teacup of medicine, this time filled almost to the brim. "Sweetheart, here is your medicine. Try to drink every last drop, and I promise you'll begin to feel much better fast."

The first sip did not seem as wonderfully scrumptious as Kim had remembered in her dream. But neither did it taste as bad as the night before. She now managed to drink the entire cup.

"That's a good girl," Verbada said. "You should be feeling better very soon. I'll tell you what we can do if you think you're up to it. We can make some of my special mud pies. Would you like that?"

"Yes," said Kim, remembering how pleasant her dream had been.

"Very good," said Verbada. "Then I shall have the kitchen prepared. You've not seen the kitchen yet, but I think you'll find it a very interesting place. Now get dressed, and I'll be back for you in about fifteen minutes."

Once Kim had dressed, Verbada returned with a package wrapped in pink and orange Widgmus paper. "This is a little present from me to you. I hope you will like it."

"Gee, thanks," said Kim, grabbing the package and tearing into it. Once she had torn the paper off the box, she opened it and found some kind of rough cloth garment inside.

"It's an apron, my dear," Verbada informed her. "You will need one so that you won't mess up your nice clothes making mud pies."

"Thanks," said Kim, and Verbada without warning lunged at her, hugged her, and planted a sloppy wet kiss on her cheek.

"I would be glad for you to call me Mom," Verbada told her. "You and I will be the best mother-and-daughter team ever. Now, let's get to the kitchen! We've got mud pies to pat!"

* * *

The children whom Prince Krissmon had cured with the snow were now in uniform and were receiving training from some of Admiral Kringle's elves. Other elves, dressed like sailors, were making plans to fight Verbada Widgmud by sea, so they were preparing to travel to the shores of Tinsel Canal where they would embark by ship in search of the *Baby Lonnie*. Prince Krissmon had told Jason that he would be needed in the sea operation Admiral Kringle would be commanding. Kringle would explain to Jason his role in the plan to rescue Kim from the *Baby Lonnie*. Riding on horseback, Prince Krissmon addressed the children and the elves.

"We shall soon face our dreaded enemy on two fronts. Many of you will know what to expect. You brave children who fought before in the battle of Mud Flats at the Black

Tower of *Civit Mund* where Verbada had Lady imprisoned will well remember how Verbada and her Widgmudgeons saw to it that your attempt to rescue Lady failed. Many of you were injured in battle with Widgmud's forces. Now we must embark on one front by sea and on the other by land. The Orphan Brigade must stage a second battle at *Civit Mund*."

"Admiral Kringle!" Prince Krissmon commanded. "The time has come for you and your elves to set sail for the battle of Tinsel Canal! We wish you the speed and protection of Tree King!"

"Aye, aye, my Prince!" Kringle saluted. "The wagons are already loaded with snowballs for the ice cannons. Once they are unloaded onto the ship, we will make all haste to battle before they melt and can no longer be used. Our victory over Verbada Widgmud will not be easy, and we must use all our strength to defeat her." Then Kringle shouted, "Sea-elves of the naval forces of Arboria! Forward to the docks of Tinsel Canal!"

"Jason," spoke Prince Krissmon. "You must go now with Admiral Kringle. He will reveal to you our strategy for rescuing your sister from Verbada's clutches."

"Aye, aye!" Jason replied.

"Ride with me, then, young man," Admiral Kringle ordered. He reached down and pulled Jason up onto his horse. "Hold tight. We must ride ahead of the others."

"Officers!" shouted Prince Krissmon. "We must begin our march to the Mud Flats to fight the second battle of *Civit Mund*! Rally the troops!"

With those words, Admiral Kringle spurred his horse and galloped out with Jason riding behind him and holding on tightly. They sped out, and the elves' naval brigade fell into formation. Wagons filled with snowballs also began pulling out.

Tinsel Canal was less than two miles from camp, and soon Admiral Kringle and Jason were galloping toward the good ship *Donna*. The vessel was large and sturdy, having three masts. Its sails were white and crimson, trimmed with holly and ivy leaf designs. From the top of the masts flew white flags embroidered with red crosses outlined in gold. When they approached the pier, Admiral Kringle and Jason leapt off their horses and hurried up the plank, boarding the ship.

"We're going to my quarters, Jason," said Admiral Kringle. "I must brief you on a top-secret plan to rescue your sister from Verbada's clutches."

As Admiral Kringle and Jason consulted in private, the elves' naval brigade began loading snowballs into the ship's ammunition bays. In a little over a half-hour, the crew had boarded the ship and were ready to set sail.

Admiral Kringle and Jason had been engaged in secret meetings for about an hour when a knock came at the Admiral's door. "Remember, Jason. Top secret. No one must know, not even the elves. We never know when Verbada's spies may be lurking about."

"Aye, aye, Admiral!" said Jason.

Kringle answered the knock at the door. The first mate stood outside. "We're ready to set sail, Admiral."

"Give the orders," said Kringle. "Jason and I will join you above board shortly."

—Chapter Twelve—

OPERATION LIGHTNING SPEED

"ALL HANDS ON DECK!" shouted Admiral Kringle, appearing above board. Jason stood beside him as he issued orders. "Helmsman, prepare to take the wheel!" The Admiral pointed to the shipmen as he issued further commands. "Loose the moorings! Anchors aweigh! Hoist up the sails! Adjust the booms!"

The crew of elves hustled, following his orders.

"Navigator!" hollered Admiral Kringle. "Set in the course!"

"Aye, aye, sir!" he replied.

As soon as the ship was readied to sail, the Admiral shouted, "Embark!" The helmsman took control of the wheel, and the ship backed steadily out of port. When there was enough leeway from the moorings, the Admiral gave the order, "Set sail!" The ship turned southward. "Full and by!" Kringle ordered.

The shipmen adjusted the booms, and the sails flapped as they filled with air. The ship picked up speed.

"Bring her to 20 knots!" Kringle shouted.

Jason held on to the bulwark near the stern, staring at the ship's wake as she cut through the waves of Tinsel Canal. The snakeskin patters of pink, orange, and green that he had earlier seen running under WidgoVision Studios appeared again.

"Follow me," Admiral Kringle motioned to him. They walked the length of the ship from stern to bow. Jason noticed that the wooden figurehead on the bow was a woman's head that donned a wreath of twelve candles. "Hey, that looks like Verbada Widgmud's head," Jason remarked, only viewing it from behind.

"You know better," Admiral Kringle corrected him. "It is the figurehead of the True Queen of Arboria, the one we call Lady. Our ship, the *Donna*, is named after her, for the name *Donna* means Lady. Verbada Widgmud is hardly a Lady. She controls and possesses people and things not belonging to her. Widgmud is the mistress of grand larceny. She stole Lady's headdress when she had Lady imprisoned at Black Tower. If I have anything to do with it, that headdress will be recovered and returned to its rightful owner as soon as the Battle of Tinsel Canal is won. But the battle will no doubt be fierce if Verbada Widgmud has her way. We are in her territory now, and I can't guarantee the waters of Tinsel Canal will allow us smooth sailing for long. She controls them just as she does her Widgmudgeons. When she gets wind of our plans, and I'm sure that may be sooner than later, we shall be in for some rough weather."

"The ship's on a straight and fast course," the Admiral said. "You and I must return to my cabin. We must prepare you to save your sister from Verbada's clutches."

* * *

Bringing his horse about to address his troops, Prince Krissmon called the Orphan Brigade to a halt. They had already begun the long march to Mud Flats about the time Admiral Kringle had set sail.

The Prince addressed them. "Troops, since we are nearing Widgmudgeon territory, we must station ourselves here until we get word that it is safe to move through. Our greatest hope for victory is that Admiral Kringle will put up a fierce enough sea battle to distract Verbada and her forces away as we make our movement toward Mud Flats. If we are right, she will have no choice but to round up most of her Widgmudgeons to shore-up her defenses. She knows she is most vulnerable to attack on Tinsel Canal. With her Widgmudgeons pulled away to help defend her, we will gain the strategic advantage of having the way to the Mud Flats cleared of the nasty creatures. If my guess is right, she will call upon them to serve as her first defense against Admiral Kringle's snow cannons. We know she will never risk her personal safety but will use her Widgmudgeons to absorb and neutralize as much of Admiral Kringle's snow reserves as possible. Remember, Verbada Widgmud's creatures are expendable since she knows she can always make more of them once the heat of battle has died down. Scouts have already been sent ahead to watch for unusual signs of movement. Meanwhile, there will be no time to set up camp. We must remain battle ready. So eat your rations and nap while there is time. As you war-hardened troops well know, you will need every ounce of strength you can muster for the battle ahead."

* * *

Kim had been busy helping Verbada sew pink sequins in the shape of lightning bolts on one of her new orange velour blouses. Verbada meanwhile had been hot-gluing pink bric-a-brac on a pair of orange vinyl boots. "These will look superb on me at the Widgmudgeon square dance next Friday," she said, holding them up and admiring her work.

"Let me see how your needlework is going, my dear," said Verbada.

Kim held the blouse up, "It looks nice, doesn't it?"

"Hmmm," Verbada responded, examining it. "I know what's missing. Your lightning strikes each need one more zigzag. Be sure there are enough to spell out my initials, V.W. That is my trademark, remember?" She gave Kim the blouse back, and Kim willingly started sewing on more sequins.

"Would you like some Widgmus eggnog, dear?" Verbada asked her.

"Yes, thank you," she replied. "Could I have an apple dumpling, too?"

"I'm afraid I will spoil you," said Verbada. "But I don't care. I'm just thrilled to death that you've learned to love my cooking. You are growing up to be a lady of very fine taste—a lady of distinction. I'll run to the galley and see if we have any apple dumplings left over. If not, I'll cook some up just for you."

As soon as Verbada had left the cabin, Kim laid down the blouse, went to Verbada's closet, and stood on tiptoe to get down the box containing Queen Lady's Susie Q. She placed it on Verbada's dressing table, opened the lid, removed it from the box, and arranged it carefully on her head. She looked at herself in the mirror, and imagined herself to be the star in one of Verbada's infomercials. "And a widgle, mudgle, jingle all the way," she sang to herself. But at that very moment, the reflection of her face in the mirror turned the color of mud, and her eyes glowed hot pink. Frightened half out of her wits, she yanked off the Susie Q, stuffed it back in the box, shut the lid, and thrust it up onto the top shelf in Verbada's closet. She crept back over to the mirror, fearing the reflection she might see. To her utter relief she appeared normal. Still terribly frightened and shaking all over, she returned to her sewing.

In a little while, Verbada returned with Widgmus eggnog and an apple dumpling. "Here's your snack, dear. I hope you enjoy these as much as I did preparing them for you."

"I've change my mind. I feel a bit sick to my stomach," said Kim.

"WHAT!" screamed Verbada. "I'LL HAVE YOU KNOW I MADE THAT APPLE DUMPLING FROM SCRATCH!"

Kim shrunk back in fear. "I'm sorry. I don't feel well."

"You don't feel well?" she screeched. "What about me? I've been using that blasted cyberbonnet all day, and my head is killing me. Do you have any idea how bad a cyberbonnet headache can be?"

Kim shook her head.

"Then you're going to find out right this minute," she yelled.

"But my stomach aches."

"HUSH!" she said, clenching her teeth and glaring.

Verbada went to her closet to fetch her cyberbonnet. "What's this?" she yelled. "Someone has been messing with my Susie Q." Her eyes threw out daggers at Kim. "It was you. Did you try on my Christmas crown?"

"No," Kim fibbed, her voice trembling.

"I can always spot a liar," Verbada said squinting. Her eyes kept spitting fire. "Now I know why you have a stomach ache. You tried on Susie Q, didn't you? Admit it. You lied."

Kim shook her head, and Verbada hurried over to her and jerked her up by the arm. "You are coming with me." Twisting Kim's arm, Verbada pushed her down into a chair and strapped her in. Kim began to cry.

"Behave yourself at once, or I'll have to dose you with some of my strong medicine," Verbada threatened.

Kim simmered down. After a few minutes, Verbada returned with her cyberbonnet. "If you think you're grown up enough to wear my Christmas crown, then I think you're grown up enough to wear my cyberbonnet, too." Verbada pushed it down hard on her head.

"Ouch," she cried, wincing.

"If you think that hurts, just wait," threatened Verbada. "My cyberbonnet is going to give your poor little brain a workout you'll never forget."

Suddenly, Kim's head started spinning and terrifying images swirled about in an eerie green glowing liquid that filled her mind. As it did, a high-pitched fevered shrill grew louder until it spiked. Radioactive pink splotches began to crackle through the liquid, sounding like electrical sparks. She could no longer see or hear anything in the room, not even Verbada's cackling. Kim couldn't breathe either. The glowing green liquid swirling in her mind made her feel as though she were drowning. She remembered that feeling from the time she and Jason first entered Widgmus World and struggled to free themselves from the waters of Tinsel Canal.

As the green liquid swirled, Kim's head ached and the pit of her stomach filled to the brim with a nauseating sense of dread. When she could stand it no more, the green liquid spun laser webs out from the cyberbonnet, and the hideous pink electrical spiders escaped from its holes. She felt slight relief until she started getting feedback from the minds of thousands of Widgmudgeons. Their thoughts assaulted her thoughts and were almost too terrible for her to bear. She began shaking uncontrollably, believing that her head might explode at any minute like the head of a Windbaggit pricked by a Needlenoggin's quill. Verbada, realizing that Kim had had enough, removed the cyberbonnet. Kim, exhausted from the ordeal, collapsed, appearing now like a zombie.

"That will teach you to mess with any of my headgear," Verbada stated cruelly. "You know now that you're not ready for my cyberbonnet, but you will be soon, my dear. The next time I make you use the device, I'll turn it on low to help you get adjusted to its extraordinary power. In time, you'll learn to control it just as I have. Now, drink some of my Widgmus eggnog and eat the apple dumpling I made for you. It will help clear your mind and soothe your headache."

Verbada fed her apple dumpling to Kim one spoonful at a time, followed by sips of Widgmus eggnog. "That's it. You will feel much better soon."

Kim's head and stomach did stop hurting, but she felt very strange, as though she were sinking into a deep, dark, silent hole. When she fell asleep, she was haunted by the memory of the Widgmudgeons' thoughts. Their voices chattered, hissed, and squealed, clouding her mind so that she could not think. In a last-ditched effort to keep her sanity, she started uttering the name of her brother. "Jason. Jason. Jason." Until she fell asleep.

When Kim awoke, it was about midnight, and she could hear Verbada screaming at the top of her lungs. "Wake up!" she yelled, breaking into Kim's room and pulling the covers off her. Quirinius Grousenot was standing there with her. "Get out of bed this minute and follow me to my ready room. We have learned that an attack is imminent. Old Red Coat is approaching from the North on Tinsel Canal. I will need all the help I can muster."

Kim followed Verbada and Grousenot as they hurried to her cabin. Verbada rushed to her closet, removed the cyberbonnet, stuck it on her head, and hurried over to her chair to concentrate.

"My spies have spotted them," she yelled. "I just hope we are not too late."

"What can I do?" asked Kim.

"You may have to help me use the cyberbonnet," said Verbada. "I will have to use all my powers to fend off Old Red Coat's attack. If I grow weary, you will have no choice but to take over."

"Please, no," Kim cried. "I can't, I can't." Tears streamed from her face.

"You will do as I say, young lady. Out of the kindness of my heart, I've adopted you as my own daughter. I've spoiled you rotten by cooking for you when you did not appreciate it. Now I ask one little favor from you, and you dare refuse me? If you do not help me, we will die! Die! Do you hear me? Now dry up that crying this minute, or Mr. Grousenot will have you punished by Widgmudgeons. I guarantee you. That will NOT be fun."

Kim sat silently as Verbada's cyberbonnet began to screech, spinning out its laser webs. The crackling of the pink electrical spiders crawling across the laser webs gave Kim the creeps.

"There is very little time to create more Widgmudgeons," said Verbada. "I must first rally the ones I have, then I will create as many as I can for the war." To the boats, little ones, she commanded with her mind, to the boats! The pink electrical spiders carried her powerful thoughts throughout the vast reaches of Widgmus World. Widgmudgeons from far and wide, in zombie-like obedience, walked the dark roads leading to Tinsel Canals, manned their boats, and began rowing in the direction of the *Baby Lonnie*. As they drew closer to Verbada's palace cruiser, their midnight chanting grew in volume and in one accord. "Your wish is our command! Queen Lady! Your wish is our command!" Over and over again, they chanted. The eerie loudness of it increased and rumbled over Tinsel Canal's dark waters. One could even hear it inside Verbada's cabin. "Yes," said Verbada, her cyberbonnet furiously spinning out its green webs as millions of the pink electrical spiders escaped from her mind over the webs into the Widgmudgeons' minds. "That's it. You, my dears, will be my first line of defense against the enemy. You will have the privilege of dying in service to your Queen."

* * *

With Jason beside him, a brave Admiral Kringle stood on the bow of the *Donna* gazing over the dark waters of Tinsel Canal through his telescope. From the *Baby Lonnie*, green laser webs were spinning out, sending pink electrical spiders everywhere. Kringle soon could barely detect the outline of boats swarming around the *Baby Lonnie* and knew at once that Verbada Widgmud had for some time been summoning her Widgmudgeons from the far and wide reaches of her empire to come to her defense. Just then, Verbada's green laser webs spun out over the horizon and began extending Southward in the direction of Mud Flats. The light from the green webs reflecting on the dark waters of Tinsel Canal was enough to reveal clearly now the dreadful image of hundreds of boats, filled to their brims with Widgmudgeons, swarming in front of the *Baby Lonnie*.

"Ye gads!" cried Admiral Kringle. "She knows we are here. But worse than that, she is now sending her energy in the direction of Mud Flats. Do you realize what that means?"

"No," replied Jason.

"She is creating more Widgmudgeons, but this time, she is not forming them from mud pies. She is creating them directly from Mud Flats. This means that they will not only be of all shapes and sizes, but they will also be more deformed than any Widgmudgeons she has previously made."

The memory of being captured by Widgmudgeons flashed through Jason's mind's eye. Those creatures were frightening enough. He could hardly fathom how dangerous Widgmudgeons made directly from the Mud Flats might be.

"This can only mean that she has found a fatal flaw in our armor," Admiral Kringle remarked. "Now when Prince Krissmon leads his Orphan Brigade to Mud Flats, they will have to fight Widgmudgeons tooth and nail when they arrive. That could prove disastrous since Widgmudgeon bites and scratches are so poisonous. The Prince and his forces may not stand a chance against the monstrosities she will create from the Mud Flats."

Jason shuddered. He recalled 'Operation Lightning Speed', the secret plan they had developed to rescue Kim from the *Baby Lonnie*. The plan would bring him face to face with Widgmudgeons. He had not fully realized until that moment that they were so poisonous, and fear plummeted like hot lead into the pit of his stomach.

"We cannot afford to waste time," remarked Admiral Kringle. "Verbada's Widgmudgeon navy will no doubt attack at first light."

"Ready the *Donna* for war!" he commanded. At that moment the crew started scrambling. Ice cannons and other artillery were manned. Members of the crew formed a transfer line to convey snowballs in the munitions store from below to above board.

"Follow me, Jason," said Admiral Kringle. "It's time for 'Operation Lightning Speed' to be set into motion."

— Chapter Thirteen —

THE BATTLE OF TINSEL CANAL

"YOU WILL HAVE TO HELP me create more Widgmudgeons with the cyberbonnet," Verbada nervously told Kim.

"I don't know how. I'm afraid," Kim whined.

"You will do as I say," Verbada ordered. "I'll start you out on low speed, and it won't be as difficult."

"But how do I create Widgmudgeons without making mud pies first."

"That will present no problem," spoke Verbada. "The only reason I made them from mud pies before now is to keep Widgmudgeons small enough so as not to frighten Widgmus World's Orna folk too severely. One with a corporate empire such as mine must at least try to keep things low key. All you need to do is send the laser webs in the direction of Mud Flats. Just think of how you would like for your Widgmudgeons to look, and your thoughts will become the pink electrical spiders that will form Widgmudgeons directly from the Mud Flats themselves." Verbada placed the cyberbonnet on Kim's head, this time more gently than she had done earlier when she was angry. "Now, the cyberbonnet is on low. Think of the kind of Widgmudgeon you would like to create."

Kim began using the cyberbonnet, and this time operating it was much easier than before. In fact, it was kind of fun. "This is not so bad," said Kim. "I know. I will make my Widgmudgeons as cute as possible."

"A bad idea," Verbada warned. "Cute Widgmudgeons will hardly strike terror in the enemy's hearts. No. You must make them look as hideous and frightening as possible. Create some itsy-bitsy ones and some gigantic ones. The more frightening you can make them appear, the stronger our defenses against the enemy will be."

Kim began to imagine horrible looking creatures. She dreamed up a hodgepodge of all shapes and sizes. Some of them had legs like centipedes or spiders. Others wiggled like snakes and salamanders. She created vulture-beaked rats, giraffes with cobra heads, duck-billed platypuses with horns, and kangaroos carrying little fiery mud-ball throwing devils in their pouches. Oh, yes, and dinosaurs! she schemed. She created crosses between a tyrannosaurus and a brachiosaurus, and between a stegosaur and a triceratops. She made several fiery mud-spewing pterodactyls, and about fifteen velociraptors ranging from the size of Japanese beetles to the size of fire-engines. And creatures out of mythology, she thought. She made a humungous Cyclops with two feet, six arms, and three horns; a cross between the flying horse Pegasus and a centaur; harpies, trolls, and gremlins; Scylla and Charybdis on each side of the door of Black Tower, and Venus fly traps lining the pathway to the door. She remembered an amoeba she had observed under a microscope at school and created a gigantic one of those. Then, for good measure, she threw in a few giant paramecia, five enormous crawling sea anemones, and an assortment of mud-monkeys ranging from gorillas to orangutans to chimpanzees to spider monkeys.

"Now give me the cyberbonnet and let me check your work," Verbada requested. "Kim, your progress is splendid, just splendid. In fact, it's exceptional. Your imagination is almost as good as my own, and now I have greater confidence than ever that you will inherit my throne."

"Thanks," said Kim.

"Are you getting the hang of the cyberbonnet now, my pet?"

"Yes," Kim replied. "Actually, I'm kind of enjoying making those creatures."

"Bravo," said Verbada. "Perhaps we could turn it up a bit. Of course, if it gets to be too much for you, or starts to give you a headache, you can adjust the controls here." Verbada showed her several buttons on the chin strap of the cyberbonnet. "I'll leave you to your work now, my sweet. I must go rally my Widgmudgeon forces to do battle. We will attack Old Red Coat at first light. "I'll teach him to mess with Widgmus World."

* * *

Because Kim was using the cyberbonnet to create Widgmudgeons, Verbada had to resort to communicating with her Widgmudgeons in a less technical way. As Verbada stood, towering ominously on the bow of the *Baby Lonnie*, over hundreds of boats of Widgmudgeons below, she bellowed in a strange tongue some kind of weird curse that only they seemed to understand. The tongue had only combinations of the letters "v" and "w," with the "w" sometimes being used as a consonant and at other times as a vowel. If she had been able to use her cyberbonnet, the crackling of the pink electrical spiders would have been the "w's" and the "v's." Occasionally, she would cackle like a witch, and "oooo" sounds would waver like the moaning of a ghost. If anyone had tried to decipher it, it would no doubt be the dots and dashes of Morse code translated into "v's" and "w's" or "oo's", with the "v's" being the dots, the "w's" and "oo's" being the dashes, and the cackles signaling the breaks between individual words. It sounded very strange, "Oovoo v-v voov-v voov-v (cackle) voo oov-v woo v-v voov voo voov-v (cackle) oovoo voov v-v oov woov voov-v v (cackle) oovoo v-v voov-v voov-v (cackle) voo-oov voov v-v oov oov-v."

After she chanted these several times whatever it was she was chanting—perhaps not so much a voodoo curse as a "voowoo" curse—the Widgmudgeons turned their boats and began rowing them in the direction of the ship of Old Red Coat, their enemy.

CHAPTER THIRTEEN

* * *

"They are on the move!" shouted Admiral Kringle, gazing through his telescope. "Crew, to your battle stations!" Elves scrambled as they manned the ice cannons and other artillery. Jason should be aboard the *Baby Lonnie* by now, Admiral Kringle thought. It should be safe to open fire on the approaching Widgmudgeon boats. "Secure all quarters! We must wait until they are in range. Then we will blast them with everything we've got."

Admiral Kringle had disguised Jason as a Widgmudgeon, and Jason had secreted himself away by rowboat shortly after they had seen green laser webs spinning out from the *Baby Lonnie* in the direction of Mud Flats. Little did the Admiral know that Kim, and not Verbada, was now the source of the laser webs he and Jason had scoped out earlier. Had he known this, he might have decided that Jason should not be taking the risk of boarding the *Baby Lonnie* but should have remained on board the *Donna* instead. In any event, Kringle had warned Jason that he might have to take measures to silence Kim in order to remove her from the *Baby Lonnie*, especially if she had too gravely fallen under Verbada's spell and resisted Jason's efforts to force her to leave the palace cruiser. Added to Jason's difficult task was the recovery of the Susan that Verbada had stolen from Lady when Verbada imprisoned her in Black Tower. This, Kringle had told Jason, was of essential importance, and he instructed Jason on what to do with the Christmas crown once he had rescued Kim.

Neither did Kringle nor Jason know of the monstrosities Kim had created from Mud Flats. Their plan was that Jason, disguised as a Widgmudgeon, would disguise Kim as a Widgmudgeon as well. Then they would travel together by rowboat in the direction of Mud Flats where they would meet up with the forces of Prince Krissmon and presumably find safety. Kringle had decided this plan would be the most favorable, because the ship *Donna* would no doubt be in the heat of battle, making Jason and Kim's return there impossible.

* * *

When Jason arrived at the *Baby Lonnie*, the Widgmudgeon forces were just beginning to be addressed by Verbada, giving him time to row around toward the stern of the ship without being noticed. Fortunately, the members of the crew were listening to Verbada reel out her strange curse, and they had forgotten to take up the rope ladder that hung from the deck near the stern of the *Baby Lonnie*. Quietly, Jason climbed the ladder on to the deck. Then he hurried to find Kim. When he found her, she was in full gear, spinning out green laser webs with Verbada's cyberbonnet. Jason couldn't believe his eyes. The sight of the laser webs and pink electrical spiders crawling from his sister's mind made him feel like an insect caught in a spider's web. He almost felt paralyzed, but he knew immediately that he had to do something to help her. Kim, who was deep in thought with her eyes closed, did not even notice he was in the room. Jason remembered where Verbada kept Lady's Christmas crown, so he quickly fetched it, put it in a bag, tied the bag to a long rope, ran back to the deck, and lowered the Christmas crown into the row boat that was moored to the side of the ship. Verbada was almost finished with her chanting. Jason did not yet know it, but he had very little time. He ran back to Verbada's cabin, ripped the cyberbonnet off Kim's head, and told her in the best Widgmudgeon voice he could imitate that Queen Lady wanted her to dress up like a Widgmudgeon in case some of Old Red Coat's forces tried to kidnap her.

"But I've got a cyberbonnet headache," Kim told Jason, thinking he was a Widgmudgeon.

"We must needs obey Queen Lady," he screeched, and he taped Kim's mouth shut so that she could not scream for help. Meanwhile, Verbada was already on her way back to the cabin to check on Kim's progress. When Verbada opened the door, she screamed.

"What are you Widgmudgeons doing in here? You're forbidden to be on the *Baby Lonnie*! You should be fighting Old Red Coat with the others! You will be taken and thrown overboard at once for this infraction of protocol!"

Kim moaned, and Jason stepped on her toes to make her hush. "Your wish is our command, Queen Lady," he replied, using his best Widgmudgeon voice.

"Hush," she yelled at him. "Grousenot! Where are you? Grousenot!" He lunged into the room. "Throw these Widgmudgeons overboard this very minute!" Grousenot immediately complied. He had only been gone seconds when Verbada realized something was amiss. She saw her cyberbonnet lying on her sofa but could not find Kim. "Kim!" she yelled. She searched her cabin and then checked Kim's quarters. "Kim! Where are you?" Thinking that Kim was hiding, she asked, "Why did you take off my cyberbonnet without my permission? Kim! Come here to me this minute!"

When Verbada could not find her, she immediately realized what had happened. "The Widgmudgeons!" she shouted, and then yelled. "Grousenot! Grousenot!" She screamed his name over and over. In time he came running. "What's the matter Queen Lady?"

"Don't 'Queen Lady' me. Where are those Widgmudgeons?"

"I threw them overboard as you ordered," Grousenot replied.

"FOOL?" she screamed. "DIDN'T YOU KNOW THAT ONE OF THEM WAS KIM? SHE'S BEEN KIDNAPPED BY ONE OF MY WIDGMUDGEONS!"

They ran above board and peered out over the port stern. There was no sign of the Widgmudgeons anywhere, and the boat that had been moored to the *Baby Lonnie* was nowhere in sight.

"They must have drowned, Queen Lady," said Grousenot.

"Or perhaps not," she said. Suddenly there was the sound of cannon fire. "Whatever might have happened to Kim, we don't have time to find out now. Old Red Coat is attacking my Widgmudgeons! Quick, Grousenot. Fetch my cyberbonnet. I must give Kim's newly created Widgmudgeons my orders!"

Verbada proceeded to the bow of the *Baby Lonnie* as Grousenot ran to her cabin, fetched her cyberbonnet, and soon returned with it.

"Here you are, Queen Lady," he said, handing it to her, but without a 'thank you' she jerked it out of his hands and strapped it on to her head. Immediately she began spinning out her green laser webs, and the pink electrical spiders crawled from her mind into the Widgmudgeons Kim had created from Mud Flats.

* * *

When Jason had rowed their boat far enough to be out of sight and earshot of Verbada and Grousenot, he removed the Christmas crown with twelve candles from the bag and tried to place it on Kim's head. Since her mouth was still taped shut, she could only make moaning sounds, so Jason removed the tape from her mouth. "What are you doing?" Kim shouted. "Who are you, and where are you taking me?"

Jason removed his Widgmudgeon mask. "It's me, Jason."

"Jason," she said, clueless. "I don't know a Jason."

"I'm your brother, silly," he said. "Has Verbada warped your mind so much that you don't even recognize your own brother?"

"Oh," she said. "You're the boy Verbada adopted that got hopelessly confused. You are not my real brother. Verbada told me."

"Verbada is a liar. Let me put this Christmas crown on your head. Then you will know the truth."

"No," shouted Kim. "I'm afraid of that thing. I tried it on before, and when I saw my face in the mirror, my face turned to mud, and my eyes glowed pink."

"Maybe that's because you saw what you turning into," said Jason. "You are safe now, but you have to put on the crown now. Verbada's brainwashed you and muddied up your brain. Lady's Christmas crown will help you see clearly again. There is still time."

Kim shivered. "I'm afraid. I don't know what will become of me without Queen Lady."

"Here!" Jason insisted. "Put on the crown! It's your only hope!"

As he leaned over to place the crown on Kim's head, she shrank back. Carefully, Jason placed the crown on her head.

Dawn was breaking, and Kim started to look over the side of the boat to catch a glimpse of her reflection in Tinsel Canal.

"Don't do that!" Jason screamed, grabbing her face and turning it away. Do you want to be scared out of your wits? Verbada's Tinsel Canal is cursed, remember? Who knows what kind of scary reflection you'll see!"

Jason pulled out a mirror. "Here. I've got a pocket mirror Prince Krissmon gave me. Look into it, and you will see yourself as he sees you."

Kim fearfully brought the mirror up to her face, expecting to see a blob of mud with glowing pink eyes. Instead she saw herself as a radiant angel. "Is this really me?" she asked Jason.

"It is you as Prince Krissmon sees you," Jason stressed. "Do you remember who I am now?"

"Jason? Jason!" she exclaimed, lunging at her brother and hugging him. "I remember. I remember. Oh, for goodness sake, I've been under Verbada's spell. I remember that, too. Oh, Jason, what have I done? What have I done? The creatures at Mud Flats! What have I done?" Kim was hysterical.

"Here, Kim," said Jason, reaching into his knapsack. "Eat this snow bread." He handed it to her. "It will give you hope."

Kim placed the snow bread in her mouth and began chewing. Her eyes filled with tears. "I'm sorry, Jason. I'm sorry."

"It's okay, Kim. You did not know how terrible Verbada Widgmud was. From now on, you and I will be fighting on the side of her enemy. There is a war to rescue Christmas, and you and I have to help fight it."

They rowed in the direction of Mud Flats, and Kim told Jason about the horrible creatures she had created, and shuddered at the thought of them. "What shall we do, Jason? Will Prince Krissmon's army be able to defeat them?"

"I'm sure everything will be fine, Kim," Jason reassured her. "Good will win out in the end."

* * *

Widgmudgeon boats drew closer to the *Donna*, and soon were within range. "Open fire!" Admiral Kringle commanded, and with that order the ice cannons began blasting snowballs into the Widgmudgeon ships. As the snowballs hit the mud creatures, they at first sizzled and then melted. The sound of their screeches grated on the ears of the *Donna*'s crew. One after another, the Widgmudgeon boats were bombarded, and one after another, Verbada's Widgmudgeons sizzled, screeched, and melted. They were defenseless against the snow, but there were so many of them that about thirty of their boats managed to surround Kringle's ship. From the vantage point of the port bow,

Widgmudgeons could be seen crawling up the side of the ship. "They are coming aboard," shouted the crewman in the crow's nest. "Hundreds of them!"

"It's time to bring the other artillery into action," shouted Admiral Kringle. When they come aboard, we must cut them down one by one.

As Widgmudgeons climbed aboard, first by five, then by ten, and then by fifty, the crew fought them with ice swords, and threw snowballs at them. Several of the crew members, who got bitten and scratched, fell ill upon the deck, but others of the crew came to the rescue and carried them to sick bay. Several Widgmudgeons headed in Admiral Kringle's direction, so he drew his ice pistol and shot them dead with snow bullets. Meanwhile, one from behind climbed on his back and a crew member came to his rescue by grinding a snowball into the Widgmudgeon's head. The Widgmudgeon immediately melted. Admiral Kringle escaped its bites and scratches but not the mud that now oozed down his back and made a puddle around his feet.

"That infernal thing ruined my best coat!" he complained. "Well, the coat's no good now," he said, removing it. He immediately pitched it overboard into Tinsel Canal, but, when the coat hit, the waters sizzled and fizzed. Whether the canal ate the coat like acid, or the coat neutralized some of the canal's evil power, no one could possibly tell.

The Widgmudgeons kept coming, and a shout rang from a crewman who had been checking the munitions store below deck. "We're running low on ammo, Admiral."

"Bring out the fishing nets!" Kringle ordered. "The crew, armed with snowballs, had a large group of the Widgmudgeons surrounded. Several other of the crew cast the nets over the Widgmudgeons and nailed the nets' edges to the deck. About ten Widgmudgeons escaped, but as they did, some of the crew pelted them with snowballs or ran them through with ice swords. The snow was now beginning to melt, and the *Donna*'s crew was running out of time.

"Quick," said Admiral Kringle. "Cast what snowballs you have evenly on the net and stomp the snow as thoroughly into the Widgmudgeons as you can."

The crew obeyed the order. They stomped on the Widgmudgeons, but a few of the crew got their legs bitten or scratched. Those who did jumped away from the large pot of Widgmudgeon mush and immediately fell ill upon the deck. When only about fifteen Widgmudgeons remained, they realized they were outnumbered and started to jump ship.

"Catch them before they escape, or they will regroup and retaliate!" Admiral Kringle shouted.

The crew managed to shoot several of them in the back with ice pistols just as they climbed onto the ships railing. No one could tell how many escaped. Some said twenty, others said thirty. What they all did realize is that the Widgmudgeons would probably wait until the crew was asleep. Then they probably would sneak aboard the ship at night and mount another attack. This was a frightening thought, since the *Donna* was down to about thirty snowballs, and these were rapidly melting.

* * *

Verbada stood on the bow of the *Baby Lonnie*, spinning out green laser webs and sending out pink electrical spiders from her cyberbonnet, and her eyes spat fire. She was enraged at what Old Red Coat's navy had done to her Widgmudgeons. Though she controlled every movement of her Widgmudgeons with her cyberbonnet, like a person playing a video game, she had lost. But she knew if she couldn't win playing by the rules, she could win by breaking the rules, and that is exactly what she decided to do. As a ploy to make Kringle think she was retreating, she called back the remaining Widgmudgeons that had survived their battle with the *Donna*.

Meanwhile, on the *Donna*, the crewman in the crow's nest spotted Widgmudgeon boats traveling back in the direction of the *Baby Lonnie*. "Look, Admiral!" he shouted. "They are in retreat!"

Immediately the crew broke into cheers and sailor caps flew upward through the air like a flock of birds. One crewman began playing an accordion; a second, a fiddle; and a third, a harmonica. The elf sailors began locking arms and dancing in circles. Someone made up a song, "What do you do with a melted 'mudgeon? What do you do with a melted 'mudgeon? What do you do with a melted 'mudgeon, early in the morning?" The merry crew joined in, and clapped their hands and sang to the top of their lungs.

About that time, the ship's doctor came above board to report the casualties to the Admiral. He whispered in the Admiral's ear, and the Admiral's smile disappeared; his face became serious.

"Attention!" he shouted. Immediately, the crew stopped its merrymaking.

"There are ten dead, and another five are not expected to make it through the day."

The crew, with somber faces, removed their caps and held them to their hearts. All were silent.

"We will bury our dead, but not in the cursed waters of Tinsel Canal if we can help it. We will use what snow we have left to preserve their bodies until we return to port."

Admiral Kringle looked about the deck at the hideous mess the Widgmudgeons had left behind. The mud was not only a painful reminder of the elves he had lost in the battle. "Sailors, I want this deck scrubbed spic and span, do you hear? I don't want a trace of Verbada's filthy mud left on my boat!" With these words, Admiral Kringle went below to sick bay. He gave the wounded sailors who were still alive medals of valor, and paid his respects to those who died defending their good cause. "The bravery and valor you showed here today will not be forgotten, my young heroes. This I promise." With these words, Kringle went to his cabin for a much needed rest, but he could not seem to get his mind off Jason and his sister. Were they safe? Were they in danger? There was no way of telling.

—Chapter Fourteen—

THE BATTLE OF MUD FLATS

THERE WAS SHOUTING and pounding on the door. "Admiral! Admiral!" Kringle jumped up to answer it. The first mate stood outside, panting. His eyes were wild with fear.

"Widgmud is doing something I've never before seen! Lightning is flashing from the *Baby Lonnie* into the waters of Tinsel Canal."

Admiral Kringle hurried up the ladder to the deck, and heard thunder crashing. He ran to the bow. When he saw the lightening, he shrank back in horror. It was one of the most frightening displays he had ever witnessed. Enormous bolts of hot pink lightning zigzagged through the darkened sky from the *Baby Lonnie* into the waters of Tinsel Canal. The waters themselves boiled something fierce as they turned from black to a luminous green. Then, just as quickly as it started, the lightning stopped. But the luminous green waters boiled more and more fiercely, until. . . . The eyes of Kringle and his crew glassed over at what they saw. Almost simultaneously, seven heads of a great dragon reared upwards to the sky. Their eyes and horns glowed hot pink, and the scales of their heads and necks flashed like green neon lights. Their tongues glowed eerie pink and slithered in an out of mouths ringed about with sharp fangs. The fire they breathed combined with the mud they spat looked like molten lava. They appeared to be vomiting it out in the direction of the *Donna*.

"Navigator!" shouted Admiral Kringle. "Set our course northward. Helmsman, turn the ship about. Adjust the sails and take us with all speed away from this danger!"

The crew hurried to get the ship on course when a wave, caused by the rearing of the dragon's heads, hit the ship. Dark storm clouds gathered rapidly above them, and lightning flashed and thunder roared. The heads surged toward the ship.

"Quick," said Admiral Kringle. "We must throw overboard every last item on the ship not bolted down. Less weight will buy us more time."

The crew scrambled first to dispose of its cargo. Next, they tossed overboard every table, chair, desk, bed, and piece of furniture they could find.

"Spare nothing!" Admiral Kringle commanded. "The ice cannons and snowballs must go as well! The crew formed a line from the munitions store below deck to above board. Waves still lapped furiously over the sides of the ship! The roaring of the dragon's heads increased in volume until it became almost deafening! Its sinister heads were moving ever closer to the ship. The crew transported the snowballs from hand to hand and heaved them into the waters of

Tinsel Canal. As they did, the waters suddenly grew calmer, and the dragon seemed for a moment to halt its advance. But the respite was only temporary.

The ship was now sailing at full speed, and the high winds coming from the direction of the *Baby Lonnie* thus far had not made them capsize. Then a wave hit the stern on the starboard side at the same time that a gale force gust of wind hit the sails, tearing them loose from their moorings. The ship was nearly turned on its side, and some of the crew fell overboard.

"They can't be saved!" shouted Admiral Kringle. "We must jettison all other unneeded weight at once!"

"Admiral, surely not the dead bodies of our crewmates!" shouted the first mate.

"We have no choice now!" Admiral Kringle yelled.

The crew wept as they hoisted the bodies of their dead comrades over the ship's railing into the turbulent waters of Tinsel Canal. Even giving them a proper burial at sea was now out of the question.

"Repair the rigging on the sails!" Admiral Kringle ordered. Scurrying elves quickly restored the sail's function.

The ship, lightened of its cargo, now began to outrun the heads of the approaching dragon. After sailing for several hours, they reached calmer waters and could no longer see them. The *Donna* seemed safe for the time being, but the war was far from over. Verbada had revealed a power few knew she possessed. What other terrible tricks did she have up her sleeve?

* * *

When Kim and Jason arrived at the Mud Flats of *Civit Mund*, the battle between the Orphan Brigade of Prince Krissmon and the horrible creatures Kim had concocted was well underway. Using slings, Krissmon's troops hurled snowballs by the hundreds at the creatures. The sound of sizzling and melting, combined with the dying screams of Kim's hideous creations was enough to chill the flesh. Krissmon himself was leading the attack, and the battle seemed at first to be faring well. The Orphan Brigade wore armor that protected them from the bites and scratches of the smaller creatures. However, the larger ones proved a fiercer foe than anyone had expected. A Cyclops reached down and picked up two orphan girls, one in each hand, and growled at the attacking forces. Some of the orphan boys managed to lure the Cyclops away from Mud Flats, and this proved a good strategy. For some reason, when any of the creatures dared to leave Mud Flats, they would immediately melt into a pool of mud. One of Kim's pterodactyl-like creatures, which flew over Mud Flats, swooped down and grasped one of the boys with its claws. About that time, the devils in the Kangaroos' pouches started throwing fiery mud balls in response to the snowballs sailing their way. Then the harpies, spiders, and different sizes of raptors started chasing the orphans away from Mud

Flats, and many had no choice but to retreat. By now, most of the creatures had somehow learned not to leave Mud Flats. Then another obstacle befell Prince Krissmon and his troops. A downpour of warm rain melted every last one of their snowballs and turned the Mud Flats into a gooey slime as with hidden patches of quicksand. Krissmon and his Brigade had no choice now but to retreat.

Prince Krissmon's army of orphans and Kim's coterie of hodgepodge beasts were now locked in stalemate, with the creatures securing Mud Flats and standing their ground and the Orphan Brigade surrounding them along Mud Flats' perimeters. All Krissmon's attempts to invade Mud Flats and gain any ground there now seemed utterly hopeless, and because the rain had softened the mud, no one dared enter.

Kim, who had been watching the spectacle, was in tears. She knew she had caused this mess. Guilt propelled her to start running in the direction of the Mud Flats screaming. "I created you! I order you to go back to the mud you came from!"

They stared at her, daring her to enter their territory. Kim was so angry that she started to run into Mud Flats and punish the creatures over which she had now lost control. But Prince Krissmon headed her off.

"Verbada is to blame, not you," Krissmon assured her. "She shouldn't have let you use her cyberbonnet. In fact, she shouldn't even have that cyberbonnet. She has gained more power than is permitted in Arboria, and she will be stopped."

"Arboria?" Kim asked.

"That's the real name of the Tree World," Jason chimed in. "Remember Verbada's 'once upon a no time' story? She just changed Arboria's name to Widgmus World so she could rule it as her empire."

"Jason is right," said Prince Krissmon. "Verbada is a usurper. She stole Lady's Christmas crown, and, by doing so, used its power to fuel her cyberbonnet. The Christmas crown is called the Susan, and to it is invested the real power to govern this land that in former days was known as Arboria."

"We have the Susan!" shouted Jason. "I'll run get it." In a few moments Jason returned with the bag and removed from it the Christmas crown he had taken from Verbada's closet. "Admiral Kringle told me, whatever I did, to find the Christmas crown and take it away from Verbada."

"This is a great victory for us," said Prince Krissmon, taking the Susan from him. "But Verbada's power will not be taken away until this crown is once more on the head of its rightful owner. And that person is still imprisoned there in Black Tower." He pointed to its pinnacle which rose far above Mud Flats. "The Susan cannot be returned to her unless we defeat your monsters, Kim, and I don't believe that the Orphan Brigade will be able to do it."

Kim could only hang her head and shake it.

"Still there is another more difficult way," Krissmon continued. "When all conventional ways of battling evil fail, there is an unconventional way, and it is the only way Verbada Widgmud can be fully defeated."

"What way is that?" Jason asked.

"We are in a stalemate now," Krissmon continued, "and we need to figure out how to gain a strategic advantage and change the status quo."

"How?" Jason asked.

"I'm the one she wants, not you children," replied Krissmon. "I'm afraid I may have to make her think she can take me prisoner. The only way for me to break this stalemate is to travel into Mud Flats and try to lure the creatures away long enough for you and some of the other boys to sneak into Black Tower and place the Christmas crown on Lady's head while Verbada and her creatures are distracted. If you succeed, you will have to light the candles quickly. Only by lighting those candles can Verbada's power be returned to Lady, the Susan's true owner. Jason, round up the bravest lads you know, and we'll share with them our strategy."

Jason ran to gather some of the boys.

"I'm the one to blame for all this," Kim told Krissmon. "Let me go in and try to distract the creatures. Maybe they will obey me, since I'm the one who made them."

"You may have made them," Krissmon said, "but that does not mean you still control them. They are under Verbada's mind-spell now."

"But I don't think Verbada would try to kill me since she adopted me as her daughter," Kim argued. "Why not let her capture me instead of you?"

"Not a good idea," Krissmon stated. "I'm sure Verbada would love to have you back, but she might just as easily kill you. Believe me. The milk of human kindness does not run in her veins."

Jason returned with the boys, and Krissmon brought them together in a huddle. "You've chosen my best men," Krissmon told Jason. The look in Prince Krissmon's eyes became steely gray, and his face, as hard as flint. "Men," he began, "I am going to risk my life to distract Verbada's Mud Brigade while you sneak into Black Tower and place the Christmas crown on Lady's head. The minute the crown is secure, you must light its candles as quickly as possible. Only in this way can Verbada's power be eliminated and rightly restored to Lady."

"We won't fail you," said Jason. "We promise."

The boys echoed Jason's sentiments.

"All right," Prince Krissmon said. "Wait until I've lured the creatures away. Then proceed with all haste to Black Tower to execute our plans."

Krissmon walked in the direction of Mud Flats. When he came to their edge, he paused a moment and then continued walking, bravely, courageously. He ran in a zigzag pattern through Mud Flats, and the mud beasts caught sight of him. As he began drawing them away from Black Tower, the boys stood at the edge of Mud Flats poised to rush in and execute their part of the plan.

Suddenly, something terrible and unexpected happened. Krissmon was zigzagging through Mud Flats when his feet got stuck in the thick goo and he tripped. The children looked on in horror as the beasts immediately took this opportunity to attack him.

"Stay where you are!" Krissmon shouted at the boys. "Whatever you do, do not venture in here."

The beasts started to scratch and bite Krissmon. They clawed at him like cats playing with a mouse before the kill. One of the spider monkeys managed to snatch the crown of holly and ivy from Krissmon's head. As if they all shared some kind of psychic connection, the orangutans, mud monkeys, chimpanzees, and gorillas rushed to have a piece of the crown. In a moment of fury, they plucked off every last one of the holly berries and ripped off the ivy leaves, hatefully stomping them into the mud as they did. Roars, howls, screeches, growls, cries, and wicked laughter filled the air, increasing in pitch until the noise became deafening. At that moment, a sinister, howling, greenish-black tornado rotated out from the direction of Tinsel Canal with great force and touched down in the midst of Mud Flats. Verbada had managed to combine all her laser webs into one enormous whip. This time dirty pink electrical tarantulas climbed down the swirling tornado, feeding Mud Flats with Verbada's evil energy, until a pool of molten lava began to boil and to glow in a circle extending from the place in Mud Flats where the tornado struck.

Meanwhile, Krissmon, who was being violently assailed by the creatures, refused to cry out for help or to show fear in any way. They screeched, growled, cackled, hissed, and howled, and piled upon him, suffocating him with their dense mud bodies. No one in the Orphan Brigade, including Jason and Kim, could bear to watch. Everyone was crying, wondering if this was indeed the end for Krissmon. When the creatures pulled away from him, the verdict was clear. His body lay there still, pale, and lifeless. The horrible creatures had indeed killed him! Kim wept uncontrollably because she knew Krissmon was murdered by the evil things she had created from her own thoughts. Then, as if this were not enough, from the pool of molten lava where the tornado had concentrated its power, an enormous dragon head emerged, the same dragon with glowing pink horns and green flashing neon scales that attacked Kringle and his men. The children quickly ran into a nearby forest and watched from behind trees as the head reared upward into the sky. Then, one after the other, six more of the dragon's heads popped out in rapid succession. Suddenly, the dragon head that appeared first zeroed in on the lifeless body of Krissmon. None of the children could bear to watch what happened next, so they turned their faces away. But they could hear as the dragon heads tore Krissmon limb from limb and devoured every last trace of him. Suddenly, the greenish-black tornado retracted back in the direction of Tinsel Canal, and the heads of the dragon, satisfied with their special feast, sank back into the lava pool.

Silence cast its deathly pall as every eye turned and looked toward Mud Flats. Even the hideous creatures watched quietly. Then, in one great and mighty chorus, the evil creatures cheered as they embraced one another and gleefully jumped up and down. However, once their celebration had begun to grow stale because they needed more hatred to fuel it, they began to peer at the children through cold and vengeful eyes. One of the creatures got brave and stuck his foot out of Mud Flats, and when nothing happened to it, he jumped out and started chasing some of orphan girls around in circles. A few more of the creatures escaped as well, and tore out in pursuit of other children. The orphans were now screaming and running for their lives.

"Kim!" Jason shouted, "We can't stay here! We've got to get back to the boat!"

But Jason had no sooner finished his words than an extraordinary thing happened. "Look!" he exclaimed, pointing upward, "snow flurries!"

The wild mud creatures Kim had made heard him and looked up in horror They realized Jason's words were true. All the creatures started running for dear life back to what they believed was the safety of Mud Flats. But merely returning there could not protect them. The snow began falling harder and harder. The creatures started screaming, squealing, sizzling, and melting. The troops of the Orphan Brigade began jumping up and down for joy. Soon a white blanket was covering the ground. The children made snowballs and started throwing them at each other. Whenever they would get hit by a snowball, they would play like Widgmudgeons and shout, "I'm melting! I'm melting!" The whole scene was hilarious. But Kim was sad.

"What are you doing?" she scolded them. "Have you already forgotten what happened to Prince Krissmon?"

The children one by one dropped their snowballs and hung their heads. The celebration turned to sadness. Why had they been so thoughtless? Krissmon had died only moments earlier, and now they were laughing and carrying on about snow.

Just then, Krissmon's steed, which had been roaming in the forest, came galloping into their midst. He reared up, neighed, and then trotted out into the center of what had been Mud Flats. No mud could any longer be seen, for snow had covered every trace of it, but what they did see was a fissure opening up in the earth. From it a bright beam of white light burst out and shone up through the falling snow all the way into the clouds. Then a white figure that shone like the sun sprung up from the fissure and mounted the steed. Immediately, the steed, too, became as brilliant as the sun.

The children in one accord cheered. Then they started chanting over and over. "Krissmon! Krissmon! Krissmon!"

Krissmon rode his white stallion into the heavens, and galloped across the clouds. Snow began to fall heavier and heavier. The flakes were the most beautiful Kim had ever seen. Never before had such an enormous snow fallen in Arboria. Like a flash of lightning, Krissmon sped off, disappearing for a time and then reappearing. He brought his steed to a halt in front of the Orphan Brigade whose mouths were hanging open in amazement. Before their very eyes, Krissmon changed back into his normal appearance. On his head was the same wreath of holly and ivy the horrible creatures had torn up and trampled into the mud.

"A great snow is getting ready to melt Verbada's mud empire once and for all," he told his troops. The children smiled at each other and looked back at Krissmon. "For all practical purposes, she has been put out of business, though there is still work to be done."

"How did you do it?" asked Jason. "We saw you die. We listened as the dragon's heads devoured you."

"She wanted me to pay her price, Jason, but what she did not realize is that my insides and the insides of the Star at Tree Top where Tree King dwells are one and the same."

"So there really is a Star at Tree Top?" asked Kim, remembering Verbada's 'once upon a no time' story.

"Yes, and if you know anything about that Star," replied Krissmon, "it may be small enough on the outside to hold in your hand, but on the inside it goes on forever and ever. Its light may be hidden so that those blinded by Verbada's

Widgmus propaganda cannot see it. But just as my snow has melted her mud, so will the light from the Star at Tree Top melt her lies and shed its light on all Arboria as it once did long ago. Widgmus World will soon be forgotten, and so will its evil creator, Verbada Widgmud.

"Now, my children, the time has come for you to be reunited with your true mother."

The orphans glanced at one another with questioning looks.

"She awaits us in Black Tower," said Krissmon. "Follow me, and together we will free her from her captivity."

— Chapter Fifteen —

A BIG CELEBRATION

THE MUD FLATS OF *CIVIT MUND* were now frozen solid and thoroughly covered over with a layer of deep snow. Prince Krissmon walked across them toward Black Tower, and the orphans followed him. The immense wooden doors to Black Tower could not hold Krissmon out now. He commanded, and they swung open. Winding stairs of stone led up to the tower's pinnacle where Lady had been held hostage by Verbada. Prince Krissmon was the first to enter. Once inside the pinnacle's chamber, he and the children saw an old woman stooped over as she sat in a rough-hewn wooden chair. Her hair was gray and straggly, and her face, wrinkled and weathered by the years, had the appearance of a shrunken head. Despair had sapped every ounce of light from her eyes, and she was hunched over in some kind of stupor. She did not notice her visitors, but merely sat, staring blankly at the floor.

"Verbada has done this to her," said Krissmon as he saw the children looking on in disappointment. "If you could have seen her before her captivity, you would have marveled at her radiant beauty."

Sadly, the children gazed at her, wondering if she was now too weak even to be removed from Black Tower. She had been there a very long and no doubt was malnourished as well as neglected.

"Kim and Jason," the Prince commanded. "Hand me the Susan."

Jason opened his knapsack, and Kim removed the Susan from it and handed it to Krissmon. He first kissed the old woman on the brow. She raised her head, and a slight smile flitted across her face. Krissmon very gently placed the crown upon the head of the old woman, and started lighting its candles. For each candle he lit, the old woman appeared to grow years and years younger. Her hair began to change from gray to brown. When the twelfth candle was lit, she did not look a day over twenty-five. After Prince Krissmon once again kissed her on the cheek, she rose up and took his hand. "How long?" she asked, gazing into his eyes.

"Forty years," he replied.

Then she saw the children. "And are these mine?" she asked.

"Yes," he answered, "and a faithful lot they are, too. Kim and Jason have come into our Tree World from outside. Though they had some difficulties with Verbada Widgmud, they are here now, and are as devoted to you as any of the others."

"The angel Gabriel, again?" asked Lady.

"Yes," Krissmon replied.

"I well remember two children named Chris and Laura visiting me here," said Lady. "I was their guide through Arboria, our Tree World. When you return to your own land, you must find them and let them tell you their story. If you cannot, I'm sure someone has written it down by now."

"We'll do that," said Kim. "You're very beautiful."

"Thank you, my dear, so are you."

"Now, children," said Krissmon. "The time has come to return Christmas to Arboria. Here are your candles. You must take the light from the Susan into the far reaches of our Tree World.

One by one, the children lit special candles that Krissmon had made for them.

"Go, children," said Lady. "Travel through Arboria with the light. These candles burn with a special fire that cannot be blown out, even by the likes of Verbada Widgmud."

Lady and Prince Krissmon, hand in hand, descended the steps of Black Tower with the children trailing after them. There, waiting for them, was the white steed, which both of them mounted. As they did, the red berries in Krissmon's crown at first turned white and then shone like brilliant stars.

"Arboria will now be safe again," said Krissmon. "Do not hide the light, but take it to every branch and level of our Tree World. It is time for our celebration at Tree Top, so we must leave you for now. Just remember. You must carry the light."

When Krissmon had finished speaking, he, Lady, and the steed again were transformed into light as brilliant as the sun, and they galloped off through the heavens. In a very short time, the brightest star anyone had ever seen appeared in the skies over Arboria. Its beauty so lit up their world that the snow that had fallen looked as if it were glowing, as though the snowflakes themselves had been transformed into crystals of light.

Jason stuck his candle in the snow for a moment and made a snowball. "Wow," he shouted, "this is the brightest snow I've ever seen!"

All the children's eyes were wide with wonder. They began to sing Christmas carols as they traveled out over the snow. As they began to take separate paths, it seemed as though the children themselves started multiplying unexplainably. No one could see them do it. It would happen that one child would be seen disappearing behind a bush and two or more would be seen emerging. So the children multiplied and multiplied, and their candle light became ever brighter. Light not only from the snow, but from the candles, was filling the world that previously had been under Verbada's dark, muddy spell.

The sound of singing could now be heard throughout all Arboria. As Kim and Jason traveled, they came at length to the town where Verbada had built WidgoVision studios, but the studio had either sunk into Tinsel Canal or been melted by the snow. They saw creatures walking about who were covered with feathers. "Isn't it great," one of them said to Jason. "Verbada's curse is ended. We are no longer Needlenoggins! We have feathers and we can fly! Look!" The former Needlenoggin took flight like an angel.

"I thought Needlenoggins hated anything having to do with air," Kim remarked to Jason.

"Well," said Jason. "It seems that this particular Needlenoggin enjoys air quite a lot."

Just then, they saw several other former Needlenoggins whose quills had turned into feathers. They, too, were flying about, singing joyfully.

"I wonder what happened to the Windbaggits," Jason remarked.

About that time, someone who looked like Baloonia Bologna rounded the corner. She no longer had a balloon for a head but looked like a fairly normal woman. "Come along honey, or we'll be late for the Christmas party," she said. Sure enough Dagmus Trench came flying around the corner after her—flying in the air that is. "I'm coming, sweetheart," Dagmus answered.

"Oh, for heaven sake," Baloonia said. "Come down off cloud nine."

Dagmus willingly returned to earth and gave Baloonia a big hug.

"I like you much better this way," said Baloonia. "You're so cuddly."

"And I like you better with a real head on your shoulders," said Dagmus.

As Kim and Jason watched, they saw other former Windbaggits and Needlenoggins walking hand in hand.

"They still look strange," Jason commented.

"Yeah," said Kim, "but at least they're happy and not arguing."

Jason and Kim then saw some of the children lighting candles and giving them to former Needlenoggins and Windbaggits. "Would you like some snow bread," a girl asked them. They happily received the snow bread and ate it.

"This is wonderfully tasty," said a former Needlenoggin woman. "Much better than thorns, nails, tacks, and stickers."

"I agree," said a former Windbaggit. "Air is so tasteless. I am so relieved to be able to eat solid food, and scrumptious food, at that!"

"What will they be called now that they are no longer Windbaggits and Needlenoggins?" Kim asked Jason.

"Featherbrains and Blockheads?" he replied. "After all, in some ways they've switched roles, right?"

"No, I don't think those names fit," Kim remarked. "Those names are as bad as 'Windbaggit' and 'Needle-noggin.'"

"Yeah, I guess you're right," said Jason. He thought a moment. "What about Featherweights for the ones that were Needlenoggins?"

"That sounds better," Kim agreed. "But what name shall give the Windbaggits now that their heads are solid?"

Both of them thought and thought, but no name came to mind. Just about that time, a former Windbaggit came up and introduced himself to Jason and Kim.

"Excuse me, sir," said Jason. "Have the Windbaggits figured out what to call themselves since they no longer have balloons for heads?"

"There's talk of it," the man replied, "but no one has decided on a suitable name."

"We've come up with a good one for the former Needlenoggins," said Jason. "Featherweights!"

"That makes sense," said the former Windbaggit. "I'll have to share it with them."

"I know," said the former Windbaggit. "How about Mindbogglers? We have found that since the air in our heads has been replaced by deep, profound, and substantial thoughts, the 'Needlenoggins', excuse me, 'Featherweights', have been following our arguments quite well. In fact, some of the Featherweights made the comment that our thinking was so profound that it was mind-boggling. We took it as a great compliment coming from them, because before now they dismissed our arguments as fog or fluff."

"Mindbogglers," said Jason. "I like it."

"So do I," Kim agreed.

"I do as well," said the former Windbaggit. "I'll have to go share it with the others. How wonderful it is to be able to

communicate with one's former enemiesand see their point. .
.Point!" he giggled. "Perhaps I shouldn't have used that
word. But there it is. A point well taken can in many respects
be as soft and comforting as a feather."

Just then a former Needlenoggin—or Featherweight—flew
up to meet Jason, Kim, and the former Windbaggit turned
Mindboggler.

"Hello, friend," said the Mindboggler. "Guess what?
These two have come up with new names for our peoples.
The Needlenoggins from here on out will be called
Featherweights, and the Windbaggits henceforth shall be
called Mindbogglers."

"Mindbogglers is good," said the Featherweight. "I've
begun to listen to some of their ideas, and they make very
good sense. And I do like the name Featherweight. After all,
we have not lost our ability to make points simply because
we have started liking air. Just think of this. Our feathers
have quills. Quills can be used to write down great thoughts.
And our Windbaggits—pardon me, Mindbogglers—now
have thoughts that are so profound, they must be written
down so that they can be learned, remembered, and
examined by future generations. I think our peoples can now
form a great partnership and learn a great deal from one
another."

"That's wonderful," said Kim. "I would love to come here
and visit in the future. I'll bet some of the greatest libraries
and universities in the world will be here someday."

"A promising proposal," said the Mindboggler.

"Indeed," the Featherweight agreed. "There will be much work to do, but together we will see a new day in this place formerly known as Widgmus World. And now it's called what?"

"Arboria," Kim and Jason said together.

"Arboria," the Featherweight and Mindboggler repeated.

At that moment, they heard the most beautiful chorus coming from the direction of the Town Hall, so they turned and walked toward the singing. Thousands of Christmas lights had been strung on its wrought iron works, and what once looked like a haunted mansion now glittered like a heavenly constellation. On the horizon of the night sky, the Star at Tree Top began radiating beautiful colors that spread through the heavens like ripples in a pond. The colors spread, and everything around them became varnished with a shiny hue. Hovering in the air, a chorus of Featherweights sang like angels. Below them, the Mindbogglers joined in, giving the music a depth of beauty equal to that of the colors that now bathed and transformed Arboria. The rainbow of color penetrated the snow as well, cascading from to the top to the bottom of the Christmas Tree World like a waterfall of colored light.

Orna folk were now everywhere in the city where Verbada's former WidgoVision studios had been. The fragile skin of many of them, which had been shattered by the teeth and claws of Verbada's evil Widgmudgeons, began magically to repair itself as the waves of color fell across them.

"Look," said Kim. "They don't seem like zombies anymore. They don't have to obey Verbada and help her make her mud pies."

The Ornas instead radiated the wonder and joy of Christmas.

"Look over there," said Jason. "Remember how I shot Verbada's secler ray at the angel stars and changed them into WidgoVision screens? They're losing their eerie green and pink glow. Can you see them? They are shining now with pure white light."

The Orna folk began walking toward the angel stars, and the angel stars welcomed them and pointed out the roads that led to the Star at Tree Top.

"Look, Jason!" Kim exclaimed. "They become shinier and more beautiful as they pass from one angel star to another. And their colors are multiplying, too. It's the most wonderful thing I've ever seen!"

The waves of color that had flowed from the Star at Tree Top were now returning to the Star as the Ornas, forming the most splendid kaleidoscopic patterns as they gradually merged into the Star. Still, waves of color continued to flow from the Star as Orna folk traveled upward to become one with Tree King, who had sent Prince Krissmon to break the spell of Verbada and her mud kingdom.

"This is so cool!" shouted Jason. "Listen to the music! It's also becoming more and more beautiful."

"What is that," said Kim, pointing at what seemed to be the tail of a comet. It grew larger and larger, and drew closer and closer.

"Santa is coming!" an Orna exclaimed. Some of the Featherweights flew up to meet him and escort him down into the town square.

"Ho! Ho! Ho! Merry Christmas!" he exclaimed.

"Hey, it's Admiral Kringle!" said Jason, running toward him. "Look! He's riding on a White Ox with golden horns! Hi, Admiral Kringle!"

"Hello, Jason. You succeeded, my dear boy. Good job. So this is your sister Kim."

Kim had followed Jason to meet Admiral Kringle.

"Yes, Kim. This is Admiral Kringle. He's Santa Claus, you know."

"I'm glad to meet you," said Kim, shaking his hand.

"We're all very glad you survived Verbada's evil spell," said Admiral Kringle. "Your brother must love you very much to risk his life to save you."

"That's true," said Kim. "Thanks again, little brother."

Jason smiled. "Why are you riding a White Ox?" he asked.

"This is not just any Ox," replied Kringle. "He is one of the guardians of the throne of Tree King. The other creatures are the Man, the Lion, and the Eagle. The Ox's presence here heralds the full growth of Arboria into a paradise of splendor and glory. When the time of the Ox is complete, then the time of the Lion will come. The Lion is really big on time travel, but since he belongs to the summer season, you will not get to find out about him. Unfortunately, you will have to leave Arboria before the time of the Lion comes."

"But can't we stay until summer?" asked Jason.

"Sorry, but I think it's time you got back to your parents," said Kringle. "The adventure with the Lion and time travel will have to be saved for whoever is next on the list to receive Gabriel's Magic Ornament, which reminds me of something. I've got to see if I can figure out the riddle of the sphinx. Our Lion inside the Star at Tree Top is a sphinx, you see, and it is said that he will devour anyone who cannot answer his riddle,"

"In that case," said Jason, "maybe leaving Arboria now is not such a bad idea. I do like the idea of time travel, though."

Kringle, who was distracted by the Star at Tree Top pointed in its direction. "How beautiful it is! Notice how it is overflowing? It can no longer contain the rejoicing going on inside. It is spilling out into all Arboria as you can well see."

They looked at the Star again, and their eyes could scarcely take in its beauty. It made tears come to their eyes, and their hearts filled up with warmth and joy.

"Well," said Admiral Kringle. "I've much to do. Presents must be brought to the Orna children and former orphans of Arboria. This year, Verbada's Widgmus Children's Fund will not go to Verbada. It will go to make the children of this world happy. Fortunately, this Ox is swifter than an angel and will take me like lightning through all Arboria's lands. And to be honest, I'm glad I don't have to ride that Lion. He scares me a bit.".

"It would be nice if you still had your ship to carry all those presents," Jason commented. "Will you still be able to use her?"

"The *Donna* was beat up pretty badly in the battle of Tinsel Canal," said Kringle, "but enough repairs have been made for her to sail one more time. I've been told that she should be ready to set sail as soon as tomorrow morning. But since the *Donna* will no longer be fighting battles, Tree King has decided that she should be retired, so I will have to find another way to deliver presents. Still, the *Donna* will make an impressive Christmas ornament for our Tree World in the future. She will forever remind us of the valuable sacrifices that were made to keep Christmas alive in Arboria."

"I would love to sail with you again at least one more time," Jason remarked.

"You will do just that," said Admiral Kringle. "There is one adventure left in the old girl, and you and Kim will be on that adventure tomorrow. The question now is how to deliver the children's gifts in the future. I can use the ox tonight, but I must return it to Tree King by morning. And since I won't have the *Donna* to carry all the gifts, perhaps some kind of sleigh would be the answer to my dilemma."

"I think that's a great idea," said Kim.

"And I suppose Alaskan huskies would be best to pull it," Kringle suggested.

"I'm sure that would be okay," said Kim. "But I think reindeer are prettier because they have such neat antlers."

"Reindeer," said Kringle stroking his beard. "Why didn't I think of that?"

Kim couldn't believe that she was the one who gave Santa Claus the idea of a reindeer-pulled sleigh, and she didn't have the heart to tell him that in their world Santa only used a ship to take gifts from Spain to Dutch children in the Netherlands, while in America he had used a sleigh pulled by reindeer for quite some time.

"Surely by next Christmas I'll have my sleigh and my reindeer in working order," Kringle told them. "One thing you can be sure of, however. I will keep wearing my new red coat with the white fur lining. When my old one was lost in Tinsel Canal, I had this new one made to remind me always of our war with Verbada. I don't want to forget how miserable she made the lives of the children of her false empire."

"Well, children, I've got presents to deliver," said Admiral Kringle, mounting the White Ox. "There's much work to be done. Christmas Eve is almost spent, and Christmas day will soon dawn in Arboria. Goodbye, children and good people of Arboria!" With that Santa flew away in a streak of light, and the choirs of Orna folk, Featherweights, and Mindbogglers broke again into song.

—Chapter Sixteen—

ONE MORE BOAT TRIP

THE STAR AT TREE TOP began growing more and more brilliant until Christmas day dawned. "Look, it's becoming as bright as the sun!" Kim exclaimed.

Jason shielded his eyes. "I hope it doesn't nova!"

"Feel that warm breeze?" Kim remarked. "It's coming from the Star's direction."

The breeze picked up, and singing Featherweights took flight and soared on the wind gusts like angel bands. Kim and Jason overheard a conversation between a Mindboggler and a Featherweight who were standing nearby.

"In all my days, I've never known anything like this!" the Mindboggler exclaimed. "Can you just imagine it? A warm Christmas day!"

"It can only mean one thing," the Featherweight replied to the Mindboggler. "Spring is arriving early in Arboria."

"Gosh," Jason remarked. "The snow is starting to melt, and we haven't even had time for a good snowball fight." He stooped over, pack snow into a snowball, and threw it at Kim.

"Stop it, Jason!" Kim scolded. "That snow may have some of Verbada's mud in it! I don't want to get dirty!"

The children watched as water from the snowmelt began trickling in the direction of Tinsel Canal. The snow melted rapidly, forming rivulets and streams.

"I've never seen anything to compare to this," the Mindboggler standing nearby said to his Featherweight friend. "I hope this thaw doesn't cause flooding. We've already had enough excitement in Arboria over the past couple of days."

The water from the melting snow began rushing over their feet, and they had to wade to higher ground to keep them dry.

"My feet are all wet," said the Featherweight. "Well, at least that horrific mud got washed out of my feathers. I'm surprised the water wasn't colder."

As the snow melted, it washed away every trace of the mud that Verbada had used to build her mud empire so that not even the slightest residue remained.

"Have you noticed that all Verbada's WidgWare Ornaments have disappeared?" Jason observed.

"You're right," she replied. "Not even mud puddles are left from where they vanished."

Jason and Kim heard laughter. Children were running through the streets, playing with their new Christmas toys. They were riding bicycles, rollerblading, sledding down a hillside, playing with footballs, baseballs, basketballs, and soccer balls. A few snowball fights were still going on.

"Watch out, you Widgmudgeon!" one boy shouted at a girl, throwing a snowball at her.

"Don't you 'Widgmudgeon' me!" the girl shouted back, returning a snowball in his direction. When it hit the boy smack dab in the forehead, he enacted a dramatic death scene, making a sizzling sound and screaming pitifully, "I'm melting, I'm melting."

The girl laughed. "See! You were the Widgmudgeon, not me!"

"I'll get you!" said the boy, chasing after her, but she was able to outrun him.

About that time, throngs of Featherweights and Mindbogglers began singing a Christmas carol. "I saw three ships go sailing by, on Christmas day, on Christmas day. I saw three ships go sailing by, on Christmas day in the morning."

Sure enough, some of the children had brought out toy ships and were sailing them in the streams running from the snow melt. Kim and Jason followed the children as their toy ships sailed toward Tinsel Canal. But just before they would enter the canal, the children would retrieve them and take them back upstream to let them float down again.

"Something is happening to the waters of Tinsel Canal," they heard a boy yell as he retrieved his ship. Jason and Kim ran to look. Its waters were turning pure and crystal clear.

No trace of the earlier snakeskin patterns was visible now, and the canal's putrid sulfuric smell had given way to the scent of freshly cut fir mingled with the smell of crushed rose petals. Suddenly they heard a fog horn and a bell ringing. Sailing from out of the north was a ship, and not a toy one. It was the *Donna* with Admiral Kringle standing on her bow. All the children stopped playing with their toy ships, ran to the banks of Tinsel Canal, and waved as Admiral Kringle entered port. Eventually the *Donna* docked, the gangplank was set in place, and Admiral Kringle came strutting down it. The children were jumping up and down and cheering as he approached.

"Merry Christmas!" he bellowed at the top of his lungs, and the children replied in fashion, "Merry Christmas, Santa!"

"The toy delivery went very well," he told them. "I didn't have to contend with Verbada Widgmud and her Widgmus Orphan Children's scam this time. The Orna folk and other inhabitants of Arboria have been very generous this year as all of you can tell by the wonderful toys you've all received. It seems the true spirit of Christmas is back, and the selfish and greedy ways of Widgmus World have vanished. At this very moment, the melt from Prince Krissmon's snow is washing away from Arboria all the pollution caused by Verbada's mud empire. Widgmud's *Baby Lonnie* is now caught in a torrent that is driving it further and further south, and Verbada is helpless to turn her palace cruiser around. Hers is one ship that will not be sailing by on Christmas day in the morning!" The children roared with laughter. "In fact, it won't be long until she and her kind are washed out of Arboria completely, never to return."

The children cheered.

"She has also lost her power completely," Kringle continued. "When the Susan was returned to Lady, Verbada's cyberbonnet stopped working. Indeed, there is no mud left in Arboria for her to use to make her Widgmudgeons either. She is completely finished, and so is her evil empire. If you listen, you can hear caroling angels spreading the news of Verbada's defeat throughout Arboria. By midday, every soul in the entire Christmas Tree World will know that Christmas is back to stay."

Everyone applauded Admiral Kringle.

"No doubt you children witnessed the light show on Christmas Eve that came from the Star at Tree Top," he continued. When Tree King welcomed Prince Krissmon and Lady's return, the angels broke forth into song. The rejoicing inside the Star was so great it could not be contained, and the color and sound of the angels' rejoicing spilled out into Arboria in a way it had never done before. The joy that overflowed into Arboria relit the angel stars, and now the Orna folk have begun their upward journey to Tree Top where their hollow insides can again be filled with the joy, light, and love of Christmas. I'm glad all of you were able to see that wonderful Christmas Eve surprise. But there is an even greater surprise to come. If you will look about you, you will already see flower buds. Springtime is coming to Arboria. Our Tree World is getting ready quite soon to burst into bloom from top to bottom."

Kim and Jason saw that Admiral Kringle had told them the truth. Rose and lily buds were beginning to form all about them.

"Now the time has come for me to sail," Kringle told the children. "I've come to take Kim and Jason back to their world. Children, I wish you both could remain here to see springtime arrive," he said, "but I must get you home to see your parents and grandparents. They are in for a surprise, and I want you to see it."

"Oh, I wish we could wait until the flowers bloom," Kim remarked.

"Believe me, you will see them bloom, and from the best vantage point possible," Kringle assured her. "But before the rush of the river becomes too fast for us to manage it, we must set sail."

Kim, Jason, and Admiral Kringle boarded the *Donna*, and turned and waved goodbye to the throng of children, Mindbogglers, Featherweights, and Orna folk who remained on the shore.

"Merry Christmas to all!" Kringle shouted, and the crowd echoed back, "Merry Christmas!"

The *Donna* pulled out of port, and Admiral Kringle informed them that they needed to hold tight to the railing.

"Have you ever been whitewater rafting?" he asked the children.

"Only once," said Jason, and Kim agreed.

"Then maybe you're up to it," Kringle told them. "The water from the snow melt has created quite a lot of whitewater. Though she's been through a great deal, the *Donna* is a well-built ship. Now she's getting ready to be put through the test of her life."

"Okay, children," said Kringle. "Hold tight to the ship's railing. We're getting ready to hit the rapids."

Sure enough, the ship soon entered the rapids and began speeding down the rushing river that had now replaced what had been the sluggish waters of Tinsel Canal. Kim and Jason began screaming and yelling with excitement.

"This is so cool!" shouted Jason.

All Kim could do was to scream at the top of her lungs.

"Hold on," said Admiral Kringle, "it won't be long before we head over the waterfall!"

"Waterfall?" Kim exclaimed.

"I promise you'll be fine," said Admiral Kringle. "Just keep hanging on. The *Donna* will get you over safely."

In the not-too-far distance, Kim and Jason could see where the waters of the former Tinsel Canal ended.

"That used to be dammed up with Verbada's mud levees," Kringle told them, "but the melt from Prince Krissmon's snow broke through them and washed them away. In a moment, we'll be going over the falls."

They drew closer and closer to the precipice of the waterfall, but they could see no whitewater at its bottom. The waterfall instead seemed to empty into oblivion. The ship began to tip downward. Kim and Jason closed their eyes and clung to the ship's railing. The ship went over the fall and plummeted, faster and faster—faster than any decline on any rollercoaster they had ever ridden—faster than skydiving. They kept screaming as they held on for dear life.

—Chapter Seventeen—

A REALLY BIG SNOW

THE CHILDREN'S EYES were shut tight, and they were still screaming when they came abruptly to a halt.

"Kim, Jason, what's wrong?" It was their mother's frantic voice. They opened their eyes to find her and their father hovering over them. The grandparents, too, had rushed over to see what the matter was.

"Jason, we're home," said Kim.

"Where else would you be?" asked Daryl. "We've been here with you all along. Why are you sitting on the floor?"

"Dad, this is serious," Jason said. "You may think we've been here with you, but we haven't. We've been in a place called Widgmus World."

"It's true," said Kim. "The golden angel ornament sucked us into the Christmas tree the minute we hung it."

"You children must have been daydreaming," Janet suggested. "Grandma and Grandpa can testify. You've been here with us the whole time."

"But it all seemed so real!" Jason exclaimed. "I don't see how it could have been a dream."

"Maybe the ornament had something to do with it," said Daryl. "Where is it?"

"We hung it on the tree, right there. . . It's gone!" shouted Kim. "What happened to it?"

They searched under the tree to see if it had fallen off, but instead of the ornament, they found an unexpected surprise.

"What is all this mess?" said Janet with a tone of disgust.

Beneath the tree was a pile of mud mixed with little crutches and bandages. On top of the mud pile was a toy boat.

"Look, it's the *Baby Lonnie*," said Jason, laughing. Kim broke into hysterics.

"And what's this?" Kim remarked. "It looks like some kind of doll made of dried mud. "Hey, it's Verbada Widgmud! Gosh, she's not only had another bad hair day, look as the state of her complexion. It looks like she forgot to take off her mud mask, and now it's full of cracks!" The children couldn't stop laughing.

"What is going on here?" Janet asked in a serious tone. "How did you get that mud under this Christmas tree without me seeing you?"

"We promise, Mom, we don't have anything to do with it," said Jason. Then he changed his mind. "Well, at least not directly."

"Look, Jason," Kim pointed. "The WidgWare Ornaments are gone! Every last one of them has disappeared! Prince

Krissmon's snow must have melted them! Maybe that's why the mud is under the tree!"

"What?" Janet exclaimed with a look of perplexity.

"Yeah, Mom," said Jason. "It looks like they've melted? How do you explain that?"

"Well, I don't know. I . . . I . . . I can't explain it."

"Mom, we tried to tell you not to put those ornaments on the tree," said Kim. "Now look at the mess they've made."

"Janet, don't you think you ought to clean that up?" Daryl suggested.

"Me! Why should I?" She hesitated. "Oh, very well."

Mom fetched a broom, dustpan, and garbage bin from the kitchen. Then she filled a mop bucket with hot soapy water and found her mop.

"This is the biggest mess I've ever seen," Janet complained. "I will NEVER buy another WidgWare ornament as long as I live. Can you imagine them melting like this? I ought to scoop up this mess and mail it right back to the manufacturer!"

The children glanced at each other and giggled.

Janet reached down and pulled the toy model of the *Baby Lonnie* out of the mud pile. "And what is this thing? I don't remember ever putting this on the tree!"

"Mom, you wouldn't believe us if we told you," said Kim. "But just so you'll know, that thing is the *Baby Lonnie*, Verbada Widgmud's palace cruiser."

"Verbada, who?" she replied. "Do you want to keep this old thing? It's rusted and covered with mud."

"Just throw it away, Mom," said Jason. "Throw it right into the trashcan, and pile as much mud on top as you can. It needs to be buried. Kim and I never want to see it again."

"And what are these itsy-bitsy crutches doing in this mud? And what are these? Are they bandages of some kind? Children, you have some explaining to do. What kind of joke do you think you've pulled?"

"Don't be upset Mom," Jason remarked. "After all, you were the one who cursed the Christmas tree by putting WidgWare on it."

"Yes," Kim agreed. "We tried to tell you, but you just wouldn't listen. All this is your fault."

"My fault?" Janet said with a frown. "I just don't understand what is going on here." She started scooping up the mud. "What is this gooey stuff made out of? It's ruining my perfectly good broom. I won't have any choice but to throw the broom away after I'm done. And I'll have to wash out the dustpan with a pressure cleaner."

Jason and Kim again went into hysterics, and Dad stood by grinning.

"Please, Janet," said Grandma. "Let me help you clean up that mess."

Together they got down with towels and started wiping up the mud. They went through about a dozen towels and had to mop the floor several times before they finally got it clean. When they finished, Janet and the children's grandmother were breathless. "I still don't understand how that mud got there." Janet examined the tree to make sure there were no remaining WidgWare ornaments. She certainly didn't want a repeat of the mud meltdown. "What happened to our balloon heads and toothpick trees?" asked Mom. She started examining some of the Featherweight and Mindboggler ornaments. "I don't remember putting these on the tree. How did these get here?"

"Believe me, Mom. It's a long story," said Kim.

Suddenly, right before Mom's eyes, a rose bud opened on the tree. "Where did that come from?" she asked with surprise.

"Look, Jason!" Kim shouted. "It's started! The roses and lilies are opening!"

"Wow!" Jason exclaimed. Beautiful red roses and irises of every color bloomed on almost every square inch of the tree.

The children, their parents, and their grandparents watched with eyes and mouths wide with amazement as their entire Christmas tree blossomed.

"That's just impossible," said Janet. "How. . .?"

Everybody was speechless at first. Then Kim interrupted the silence. "It means that Lady and Prince Krissmon now reign inside the Star at Tree Top. Verbada Widgmud and her mud world have been washed out of the Christmas Tree World. Arboria is safe again."

The smell of the roses and lilies filled the house, covering up all remaining traces of the sulfuric stench the mud had reeked of just minutes earlier.

Janet was investigating the branches of the Christmas tree, trying to figure out how a spruce could blossom with fresh roses and lilies. "Daryl, is this one of your Christmas surprises?" she asked. "How did you do it?"

"I'm not the one," said Daryl. "There can only be one explanation. The Christmas ornament was magical, just as the children said. Our children really did take an adventure inside our Christmas tree. I suppose we ought to let them tell us the whole story."

"Surely you can't believe that ornament was really magical," said Janet.

"I wouldn't believe it except for the mud, the unexplained new ornaments, the flowers, and the fact that the golden angel has disappeared just as I was told it would," said Dad. I'm sure if we were to search the old church in Bethlehem where it came from, we would no doubt find it there."

Janet started looking for the ornament again.

"You might as well give up, Mom," said Jason. "Dad's right. The ornament has disappeared."

"Yes," said Kim. "Its magic power took us into the tree and brought us home again. It only gives one Christmas dream. Then it vanishes and returns to the church in Bethlehem just as Dad said. It has to return to the church before it can make its way back into the world and give Christmas dreams to other children."

"All right, if you insist," said Janet, scratching her head. "Anyway, it's time that we had something to eat. I'm sure your Dad is hungry. I've made some apple dumplings."

"Nooo!" Kim and Jason shouted, wrinkling their nose.

"You don't have to eat them," she said, grimacing. "I wouldn't dream of forcing my delicious dumplings on the likes of you, even if I did get it right off the cooking channel."

The children watched as their father, grandmother, and grandfather tasted their mother's apple dumplings.

Daryl and his parents squinted, and their mouths puckered. "Honey," he said, "I think this may need more sugar. They're pretty sour."

Grandma and Grandpa said nothing, but they chose not to eat another bite.

"Let me have a taste," said Janet, sliding some into her mouth. She made a face and spit it out. "I don't know what could have gone wrong. The recipe sounded so good. Maybe I shouldn't have added so much apple cider vinegar."

Grandma raised her eyebrow, and the children giggled.

"I suppose the only thing these are good for now is the trashcan." Janet scooped the apple dumplings from the pan and dumped them into the trashcan right on top of the mud she had cleaned up earlier.

"I'm sorry, Daryl, but it seems I've made a mess out of your homecoming." A tear slipped from Janet's left eye.

"Oh, honey, that's okay," said Daryl, giving her a big hug and a kiss. "The main thing is that we are together this Christmas. That's all that really matters, isn't it?"

"I suppose," said Janet. "You're right, of course."

* * *

Later that evening, the children told their parents and grandparents the tale of their adventures in Widgmus World. The adults were perplexed. They couldn't believe the children were able to spin such a yarn when they had had so little time to make it up.

"That's a really fantastic story," said Dad. "But I think it's time for us to catch up on what's happening in the real world." He flipped on the television with his remote and surfed to the news channel.

Daryl and Janet sat next to one another on the sofa, and the children cuddled up to them. Grandma was busy doing needle work, and Grandpa sat reading his newspaper in the easy chair.

When the news channel came on, images of the old church in Bethlehem were flashing across the screen.

"Hey!" said Daryl. "That's the Church of the Nativity where I got shot. That's where I found the magic ornament!"

"Can you see the magic ornament, Dad?" Jason yelled. "Did it get back to the church?"

Daryl shushed him.

"Early this morning," the TV broadcaster spoke, "a break finally came in the standoff between U.N. troops and the kidnappers who had managed to occupy the Church of the Nativity for over two weeks."

"Good!" said Daryl, sitting forward and watching intently.

The broadcaster continued: "A spokesperson for KRNGL television indicated that the kidnappers had run out of food and water and were weary from weeks of being holed up in the church. They surrendered to authorities early this morning unconditionally and without any shots being fired. The kidnappers, who were arrested and now have been incarcerated, are charged with illegal occupation of a place of worship, vandalism to church property, kidnapping, extortion, and attempted murder. Sgt. Daryl Jeffery. . ."

"Hey, it's you Dad!" the kids shouted, standing up and pointing at the TV screen.

"Hush!" said Janet.

". . .narrowly escaped death when he was wounded by a bullet that originated from inside the church. The kidnappers, who had been holding this old woman hostage"—her picture flashed across the screen—"released her to safety. The old woman apparently was shaken by the ordeal but physically unharmed. The kidnappers are now in custody awaiting trial."

"That's very good news," Daryl exclaimed. "This makes my Christmas complete, knowing that the job I started is finished and that the hostage is safe."

The children, however, watched in amazement, for the old woman in the picture that flashed across the screen looked exactly like Lady before Prince Krissmon made her grow younger by lighting her candles.

"Could that be Lady?" Jason asked Kim.

"It looks exactly like her," she answered.

"So Lady really was held hostage after all, not just in the Christmas Tree World, but in our world, too?" Jason asked.

"I don't know," said Kim, "it makes you wonder, doesn't it?"

"Dad, did you know the old woman?" Jason asked.

"No," he replied. "But for many in Bethlehem she became a symbol of the survival of the true spirit of Christmas. Witnesses said that she went every day to the church to pray, and was probably praying when the church was overrun by the evil men who took her hostage. Of course, thousands come every year to the Church of the Nativity to celebrate the birth of the Christ child, but this year, there could be no celebration because of the danger posed by the kidnappers. Christmas at the Church of the Nativity in Bethlehem had to be canceled for the first time since the birth of Jesus over two thousand years ago. People in Bethlehem saw the kidnappers' occupation of the church as one of the worst assaults on Christmas ever."

"That makes sense," said Kim. "In Arboria, Lady was held hostage and had to be set free by Prince Krissmon. Verbada's evil mud creatures killed him, but when everything seemed lost, Prince Krissmon came back to life and triumphed over them with his snow that fell when he let them take him prisoner."

"Maybe there is hope now that the true spirit of Christmas will survive everywhere," said Daryl. "The true spirit of Christmas was not only held hostage in Bethlehem and in your Christmas Tree World; it is still being held hostage all over our world by individuals who would change it into a holiday that is all about greed and money-making rather than about love and the spirit of giving."

"So does this mean that we will still have to battle the Verbada Widgmuds of our world who are holding Christmas hostage?" asked Jason.

"In a way," replied Daryl. "But we cannot fight them with the dark mud of meanness and hatefulness. We have to battle them with the bright snow of love just as your Prince Krissmon did. And to bring about a really big snow means that a lot of people will need to wash the mud of greed and selfishness right out of their own minds and hearts as well."

"Dad is right," Mom interrupted. "While I was decorating the Christmas tree with WidgWare, he was putting his own life at risk to help free that poor old woman from those kidnappers."

"But you had no way of knowing the WidgWare was bad, Mom, even though it was very ugly," Jason said, trying to make her feel better.

"Jason's right, sweetheart," Grandma said to Janet. "I remember the time that I tried to flock our aluminum Christmas tree with artificial snow and melted the branches right off. I completely ruined our aluminum tree. We all know what it's like to have meltdown experiences, but when they happen at Christmas, they seem so much worse than at other times."

"Yes, I suppose one can expect meltdowns to come with the job of being a mother and a wife," said Janet. "But I think I could stomach a snow meltdown more than a mud meltdown any day. At any rate, next Christmas, I, for one, won't be buying WidgWare or any similar product for our Christmas tree, no matter how popular it may be."

"Mom, are we still going to take the food and toys to the children's home tomorrow morning?" asked Kim.

"Oh, that's right," Janet remembered. "Yes, of course we are. With all this mud mess, I had almost forgotten. And I'm in charge of the ladies who are taking food and gifts."

"There, you see?" said Daryl. "Your mom is starting a snowstorm of her own. How many ladies did you say were going with you?"

"Oh, only about twenty this year," said Janet. "But the great news is that most of them have agreed to help tutor the kids in reading, math, science, and history on a weekly basis throughout the whole of the New Year."

"You see, kids! That is the kind of REALLY BIG SNOW I'm talking about!" Dad exclaimed.

Grandpa, who had dozed off in the chair, awoke, startled. "Snow? Did somebody say SNOW?"

Everybody laughed.

"Yes, Dad!" Daryl shouted. "A REALLY BIG SNOW!"

— THE END—

About the Author

RANDALL BUSH is a Professor of Philosophy and the former Director of the Interdisciplinary Honors Program at Union University in Jackson, Tennessee. An ordained Baptist minister, he holds a Bachelor of Arts degree from Howard Payne University in Brownwood, Texas; the Master of Divinity and Doctor of Philosophy degrees from Southwestern Baptist Theological Seminary in Fort Worth, Texas; a Doctor of Philosophy degree from the University of Oxford in England; and studied at the University of Texas; and for a brief time in Germany. For five years, he was a Professor of Bible at his college alma mater where he also served for one year as Vice President for Student Affairs. Upon returning from his doctoral studies in Great Britain, he served as Rockwell Visiting Theologian at the University of Houston before coming to teach at Union in 1991. He also taught ninth-grade English at Lamar High School in Houston, Texas, and served as an adjunct Professor of Philosophy in the Houston Community College and the North Harris County College systems. He is the father of two grown and married children, Chris and Laura, and now resides in Jackson, Tennessee with Cindy, his wife of 36 years.

Bush's other life experiences have included attending the Houston Conservatory of Music, playing first-chair first trumpet in his high school band, hymn-writing, extensive travel, doing mission work in the Houston inner city, living on a West Texas ranch, and serving as a part-time minister in a British Baptist church. He has also served numerous churches as a Sunday School teacher, a church pianist, a church organist, a minister to youth, a minister of music, a minister of education, and an interim pastor.

CPSIA information can be obtained at www.ICGtesting.com
Printed in the USA
LVOW031253301111

257157LV00003B/4/P